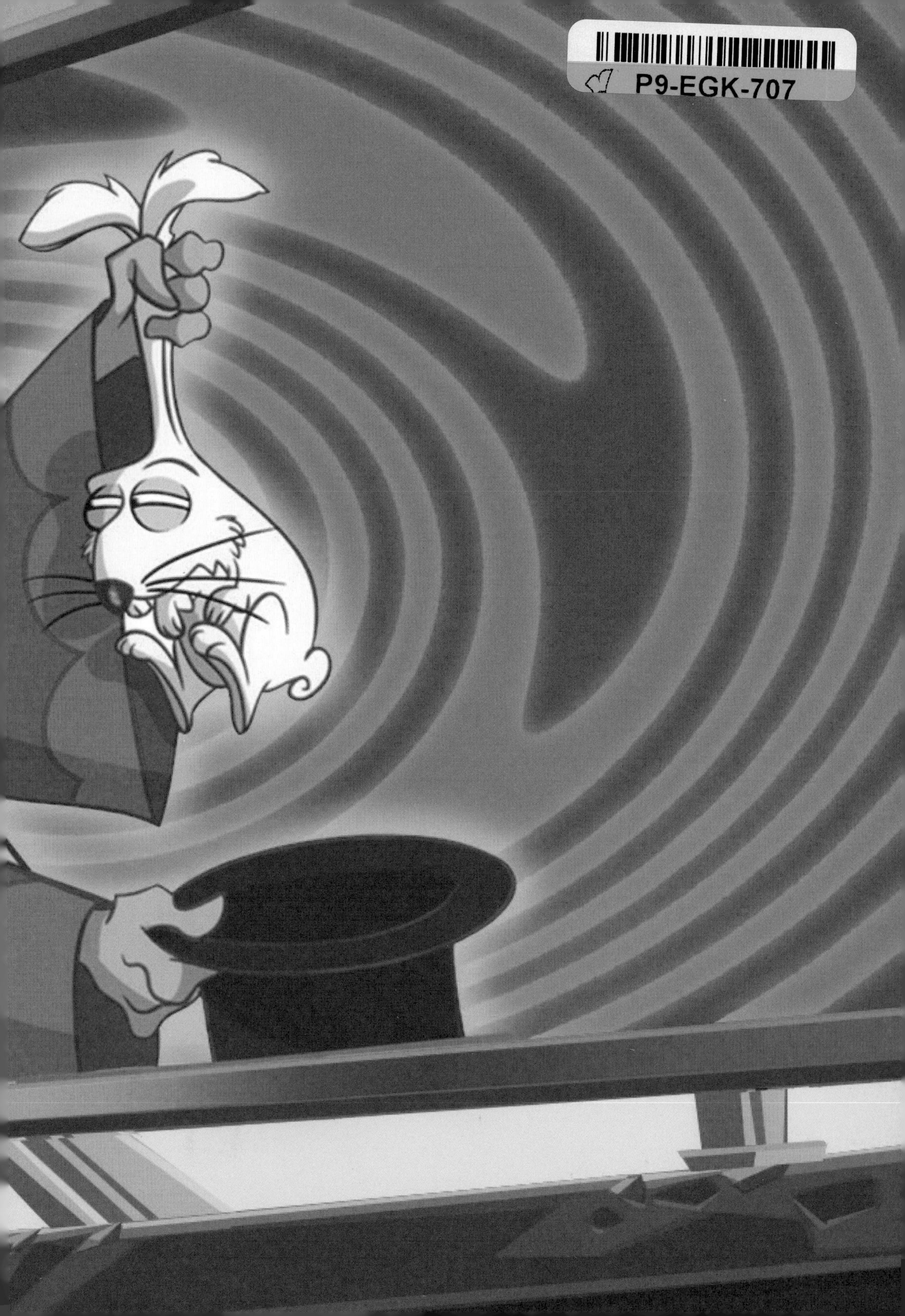

# Geronimo Stilton™ Reporter

PAPERCUTZ™

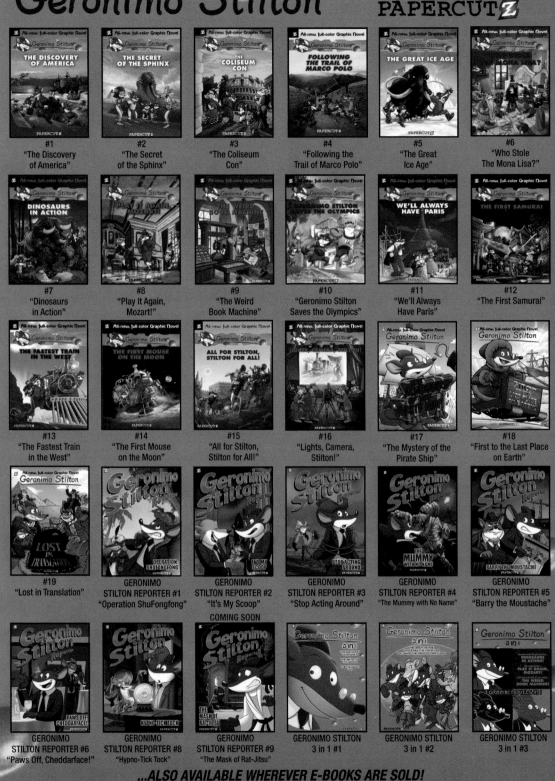

# Geronimo Stilton

GRAPHIC NOVELS AVAILABLE FROM PAPERCUTZ

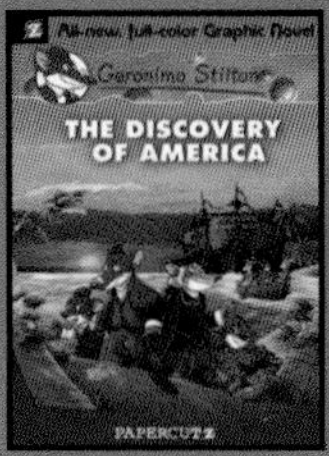
All-new, full-color Graphic Novel
Geronimo Stilton
THE DISCOVERY OF AMERICA
PAPERCUTZ

#1
"The Discovery of America"

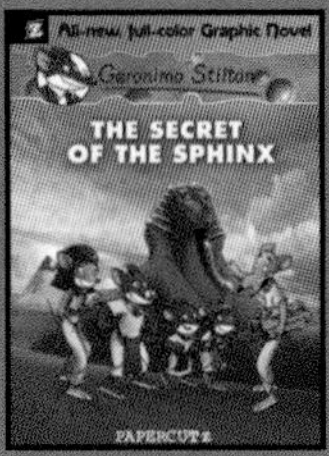
All-new, full-color Graphic Novel
Geronimo Stilton
THE SECRET OF THE SPHINX
PAPERCUTZ

#2
"The Secret of the Sphinx"

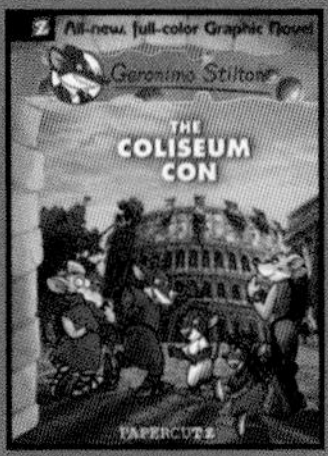
All-new, full-color Graphic Novel
Geronimo Stilton
THE COLISEUM CON
PAPERCUTZ

#3
"The Coliseum Con"

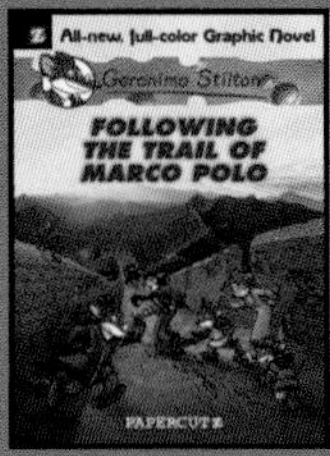
All-new, full-color Graphic Novel
Geronimo Stilton
FOLLOWING THE TRAIL OF MARCO POLO
PAPERCUTZ

#4
"Following the Trail of Marco Polo"

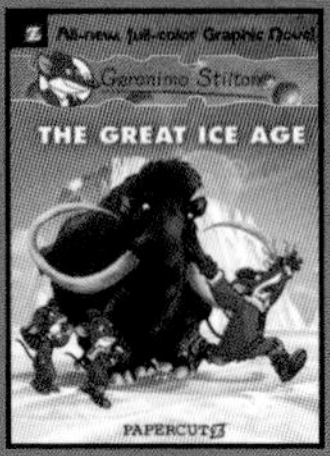
All-new, full-color Graphic Novel
Geronimo Stilton
THE GREAT ICE AGE
PAPERCUTZ

#5
"The Great Ice Age"

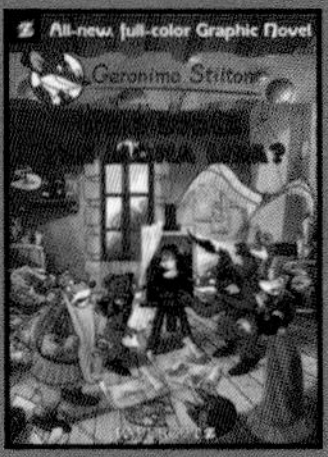
All-new, full-color Graphic Novel
Geronimo Stilton

#6
"Who Stole The Mona Lisa?"

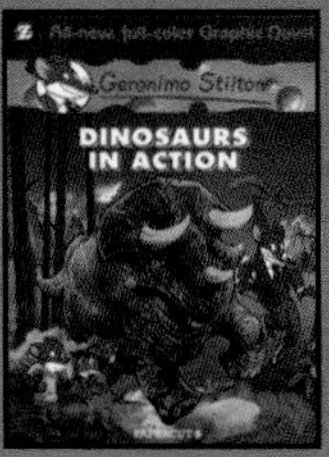
All-new, full-color Graphic Novel
Geronimo Stilton
DINOSAURS IN ACTION

#7
"Dinosaurs in Action"

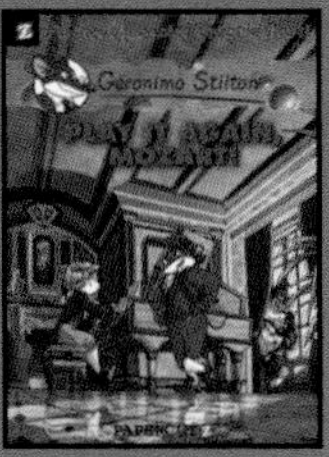
Geronimo Stilton

#8
"Play It Again, Mozart!"

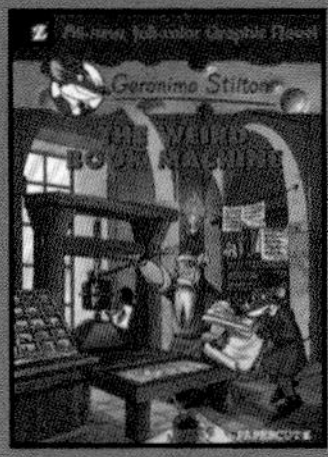
Geronimo Stilton

#9
"The Weird Book Machine"

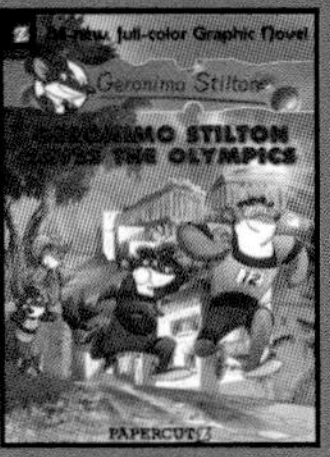
All-new, full-color Graphic Novel
Geronimo Stilton

#10
"Geronimo Stilton Saves the Olympics"

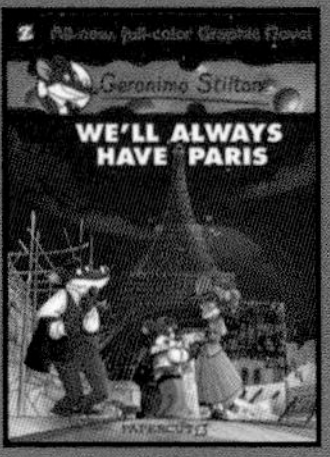
All-new, full-color Graphic Novel
Geronimo Stilton
WE'LL ALWAYS HAVE PARIS

#11
"We'll Always Have Paris"

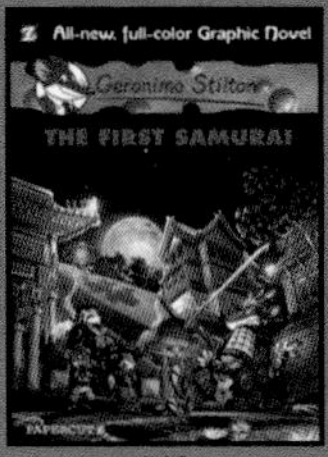
All-new, full-color Graphic Novel
Geronimo Stilton
THE FIRST SAMURAI

#12
"The First Samurai"

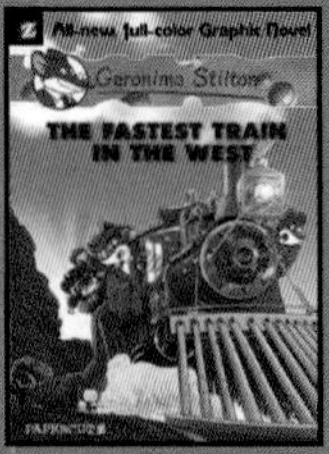
All-new, full-color Graphic Novel
Geronimo Stilton
THE FASTEST TRAIN IN THE WEST
PAPERCUTZ

#13
"The Fastest Train in the West"

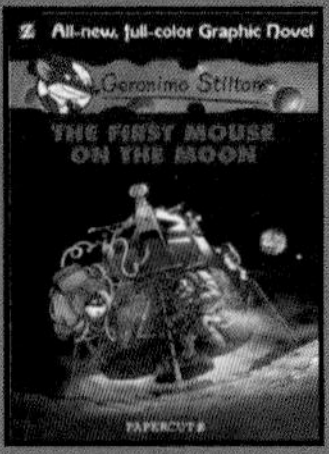
All-new, full-color Graphic Novel
Geronimo Stilton
THE FIRST MOUSE ON THE MOON
PAPERCUTZ

#14
"The First Mouse on the Moon"

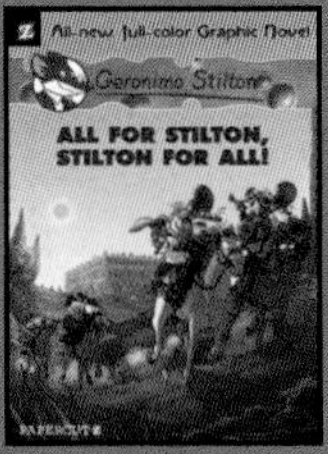
All-new, full-color Graphic Novel
Geronimo Stilton
ALL FOR STILTON, STILTON FOR ALL!
PAPERCUTZ

#15
"All for Stilton, Stilton for All!"

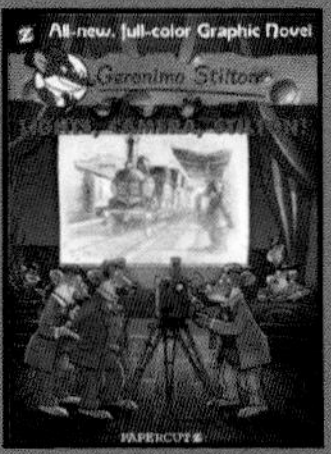
All-new, full-color Graphic Novel
Geronimo Stilton

#16
"Lights, Camera, Stilton!"

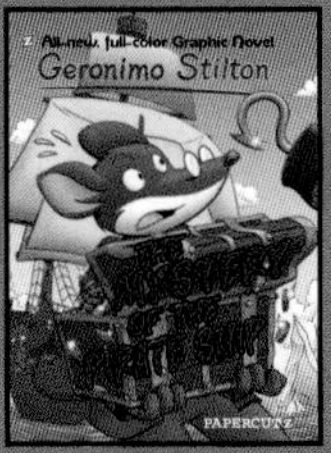
All-new, full-color Graphic Novel
Geronimo Stilton
PAPERCUTZ

#17
"The Mystery of the Pirate Ship"

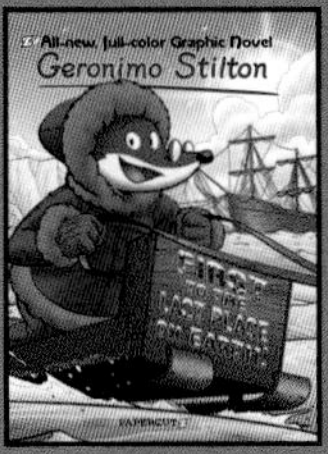
All-new, full-color Graphic Novel
Geronimo Stilton

#18
"First to the Last Place on Earth"

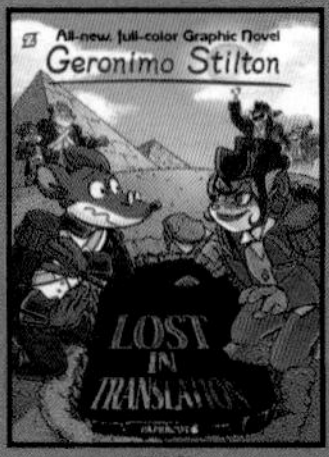
All-new, full-color Graphic Novel
Geronimo Stilton
LOST IN TRANSLATION

#19
"Lost in Translation"

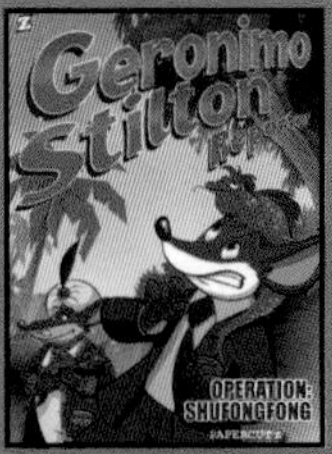
Geronimo Stilton
OPERATION: SHUFONGFONG

GERONIMO STILTON REPORTER #1
"Operation ShuFongfong"

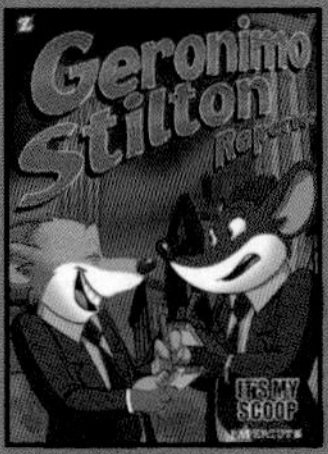
Geronimo Stilton
IT'S MY SCOOP

GERONIMO STILTON REPORTER #2
"It's My Scoop"

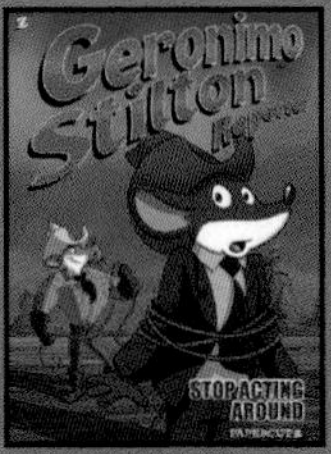
Geronimo Stilton
STOP ACTING AROUND

GERONIMO STILTON REPORTER #3
"Stop Acting Around"

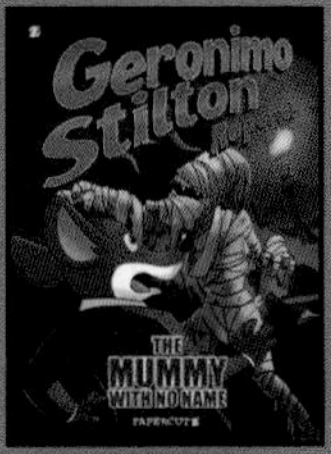
Geronimo Stilton
THE MUMMY WITH NO NAME

GERONIMO STILTON REPORTER #4
"The Mummy with No Name"

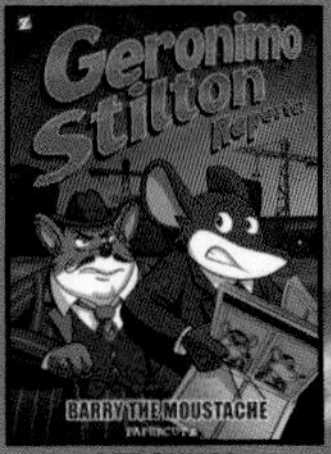
Geronimo Stilton
BARRY THE MOUSTACHE

GERONIMO STILTON REPORTER #5
"Barry the Moustache"

COMING SOON

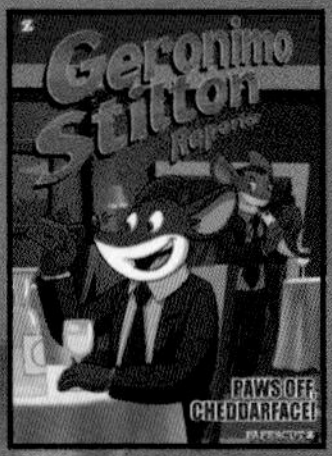
Geronimo Stilton
PAWS OFF, CHEDDARFACE!

GERONIMO STILTON REPORTER #6
"Paws Off, Cheddarface!"

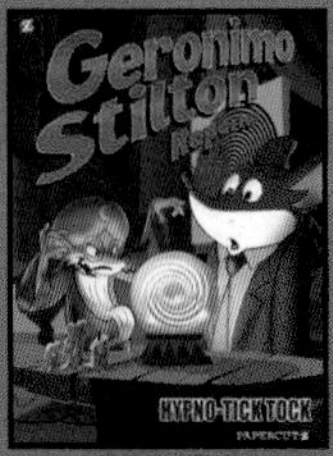
Geronimo Stilton
HYPNO-TICK TOCK

GERONIMO STILTON REPORTER #8
"Hypno-Tick Tock"

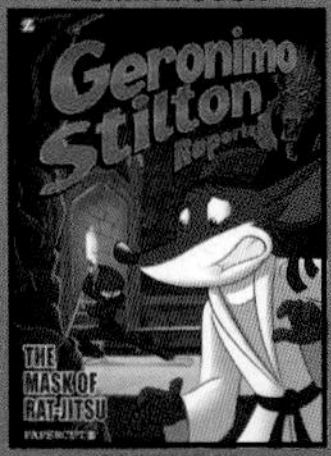
Geronimo Stilton
THE MASK OF RAT-JITSU

GERONIMO STILTON REPORTER #9
"The Mask of Rat-Jitsu"

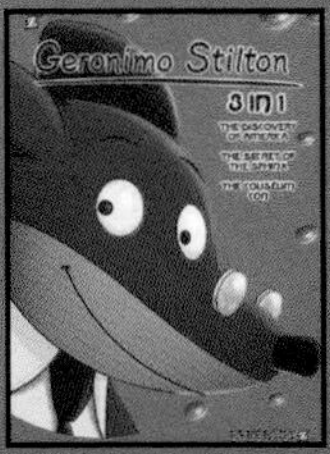
Geronimo Stilton
3 IN 1

GERONIMO STILTON 3 in 1 #1

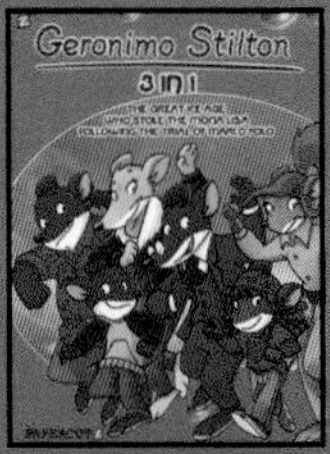
Geronimo Stilton
3 IN 1

GERONIMO STILTON 3 in 1 #2

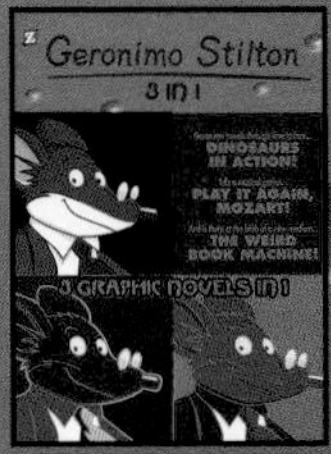
Geronimo Stilton
3 IN 1
DINOSAURS IN ACTION!
PLAY IT AGAIN, MOZART!
THE WEIRD BOOK MACHINE!
3 GRAPHIC NOVELS IN 1

GERONIMO STILTON 3 in 1 #3

...ALSO AVAILABLE WHEREVER E-BOOKS ARE SOLD!

See more at papercutz.com

# Geronimo Stilton™ Reporter

## #8 HYPNO-TICK TOCK
## By Geronimo Stilton

PAPERCUTZ™

NEW YORK

HYPNO-TICK TOCK
Geronimo Stilton names, characters and related indicia are copyright, trademark and exclusive license of Atlantyca S.p.A.
All right reserved.
The moral right of the author has been asserted.

Text by Geronimo Stilton
Cover by ALESSANDRO MUSCILLO (artist) and CHRISTIAN ALIPRANDI (colorist)
Editorial supervision by ALESSANDRA BERELLO (Atlantyca S.p.A.)
Editing by ANITA DENTI (Atlantyca S.p.A.)
Script by DARIO SICCHIO
Art by ALESSANDRO MUSCILLO
Color by CHRISTIAN ALIPRANDI
Original Lettering by MARIA LETIZIA MIRABELLA

Special thanks to CARMEN CASTILLO

TM & © Atlantyca S.p.A. Animated Series © 2010 Atlantyca S.p.A.– All Rights Reserved
International Rights © Atlantyca S.p.A., via Leopardi 8 - 20123 Milano - Italia - foreignrights@atlantyca.it - www.atlantyca.com
© 2021 for this Work in English language by Papercutz, 160 Broadway, Suite 700, East Wing, New York, NY 10038
www.papercutz.com

Based on an original idea by ELISABETTA DAMI.
Based on episode 8 of the Geronimo Stilton animated series "A me gli occhi," ["Hypno-Tick Tock"] written by CHARLOTTE
FULLERTON, storyboard by PIER DI GIÀ & PATRIZIA NASI
Preview based on episode 9 of the Geronimo Stilton animated series "Il Gran Torneo dei Guerrieri Topitsu," ["The Mask of the Rat-
Jitsu"] written by DIANE MOREL, storyboard by JEAN TEXIER
www.geronimostilton.com

Stilton is the name of a famous English cheese. It is a registered trademark of the Stilton Cheese Makers' Association.
For more information go to www.stiltoncheese.com

JAYJAY JACKSON — Production
WILSON RAMOS JR. — Lettering
JEFF WHITMAN — Managing Editor
INGRID RIOS — Editorial Intern
JIM SALICRUP
Editor-in-Chief

ISBN: 978-1-5458-0699-9

Printed in China
July 2021

Papercutz books may be purchased for business or promotional use.
For information on bulk purchases please contact
Macmillan Corporate and Premium Sales
Department at (800) 221-7945x5442.

Distributed by Macmillan
First Printing

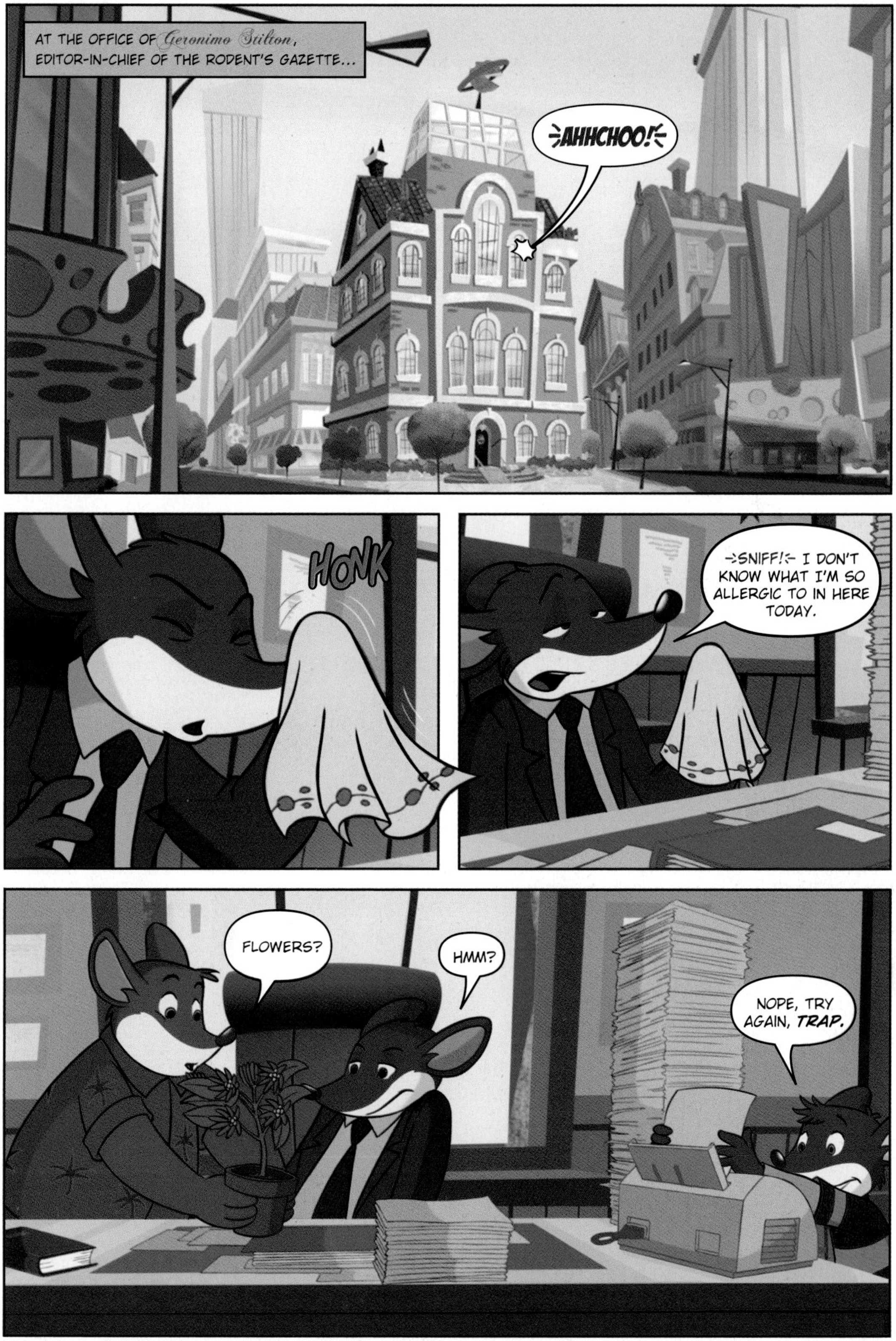
AT THE OFFICE OF Geronimo Stilton, EDITOR-IN-CHIEF OF THE RODENT'S GAZETTE...
AHHCHOO!
HONK
SNIFF! I DON'T KNOW WHAT I'M SO ALLERGIC TO IN HERE TODAY.
FLOWERS?
HMM?
NOPE, TRY AGAIN, TRAP.

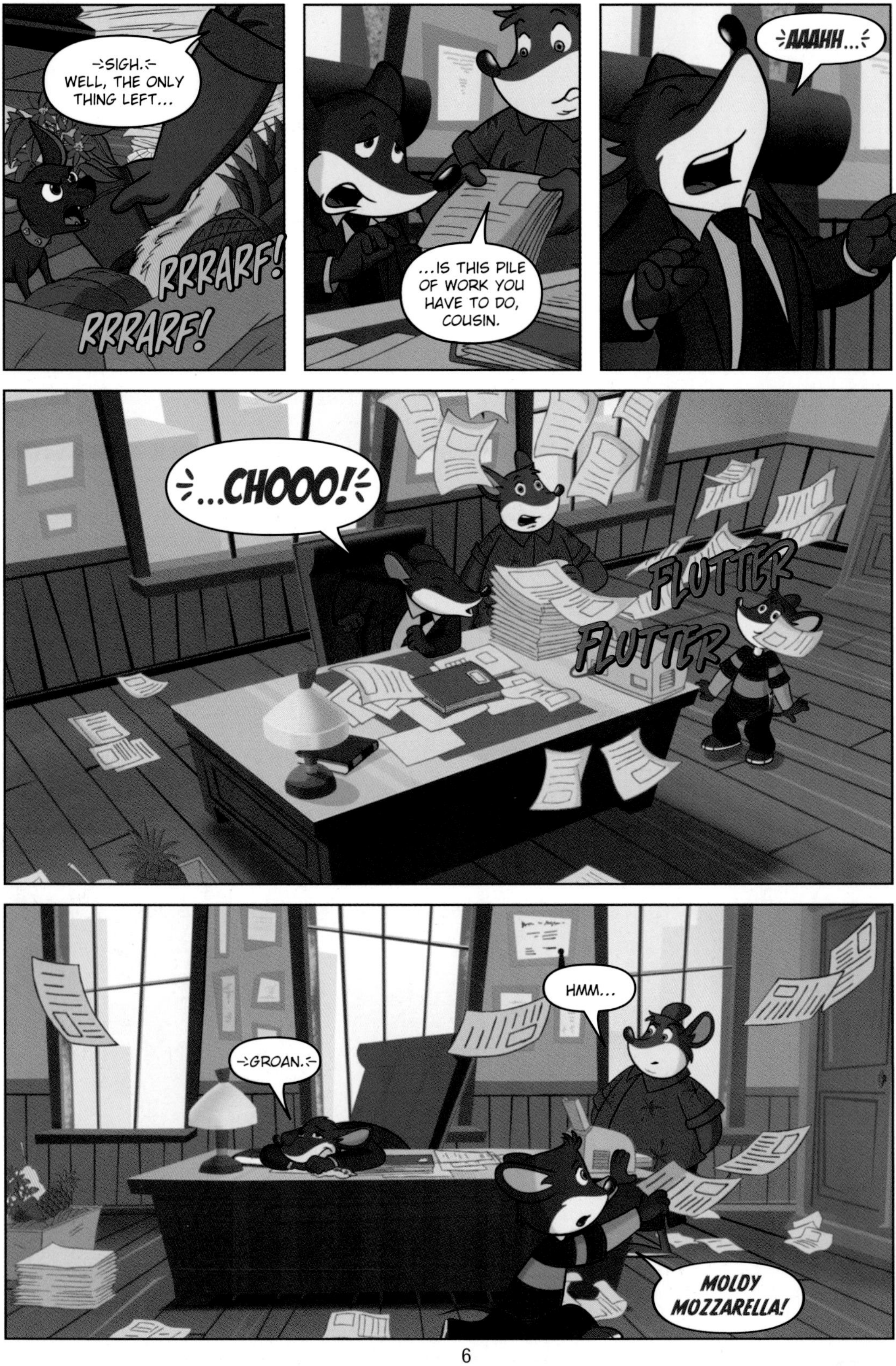

SIGH.
WELL, THE ONLY THING LEFT...
RRRARF!
RRRARF!
...IS THIS PILE OF WORK YOU HAVE TO DO, COUSIN.
AAAHH...
...CHOOO!
FLUTTER
FLUTTER
HMM...
GROAN.
MOLDY MOZZARELLA!

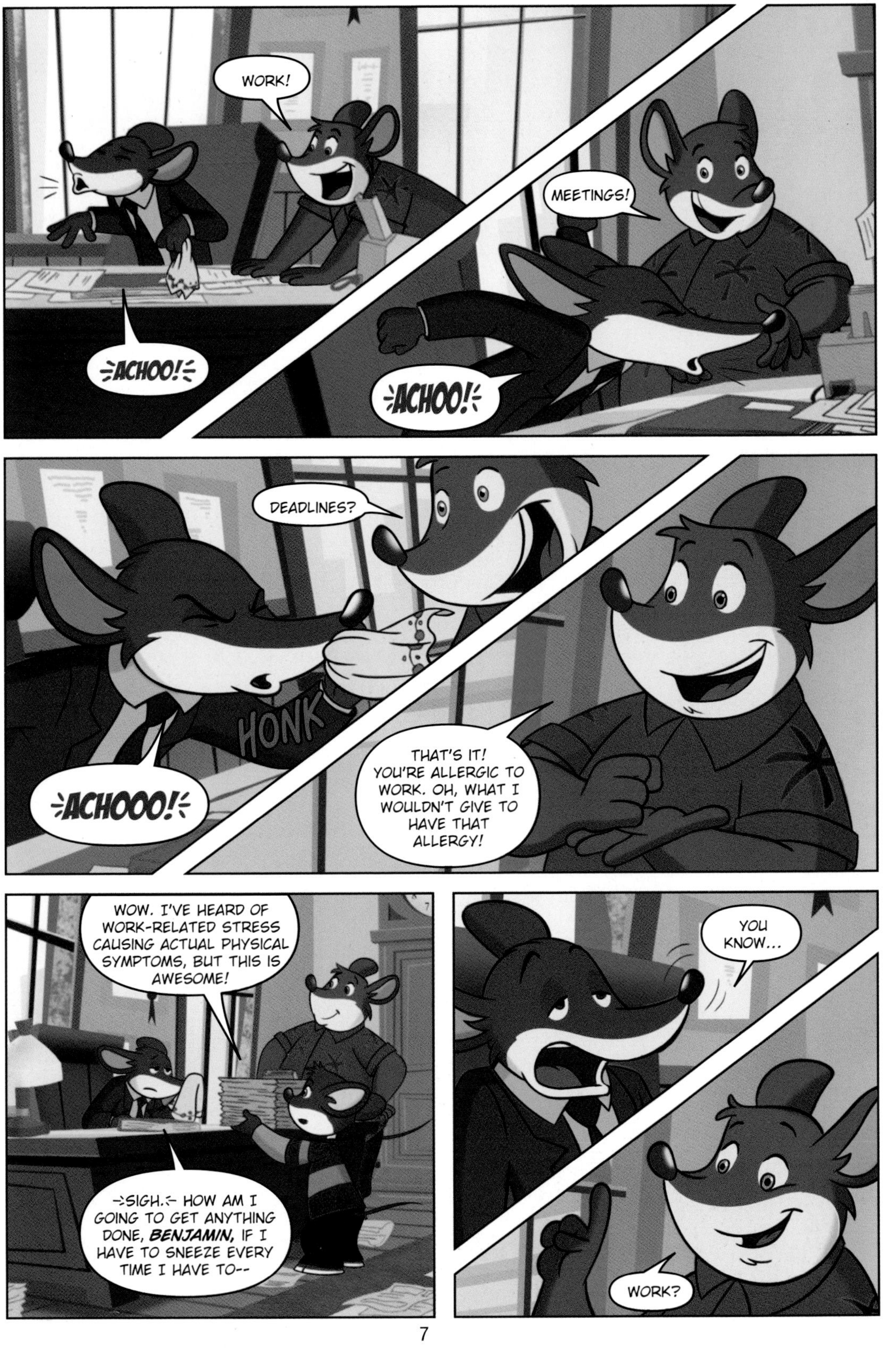
WORK!
ACHOO!
MEETINGS!
ACHOO!
DEADLINES?
HONK
ACHOOO!
THAT'S IT! YOU'RE ALLERGIC TO WORK. OH, WHAT I WOULDN'T GIVE TO HAVE THAT ALLERGY!
WOW. I'VE HEARD OF WORK-RELATED STRESS CAUSING ACTUAL PHYSICAL SYMPTOMS, BUT THIS IS AWESOME!
SIGH. HOW AM I GOING TO GET ANYTHING DONE, BENJAMIN, IF I HAVE TO SNEEZE EVERY TIME I HAVE TO--
YOU KNOW...
WORK?

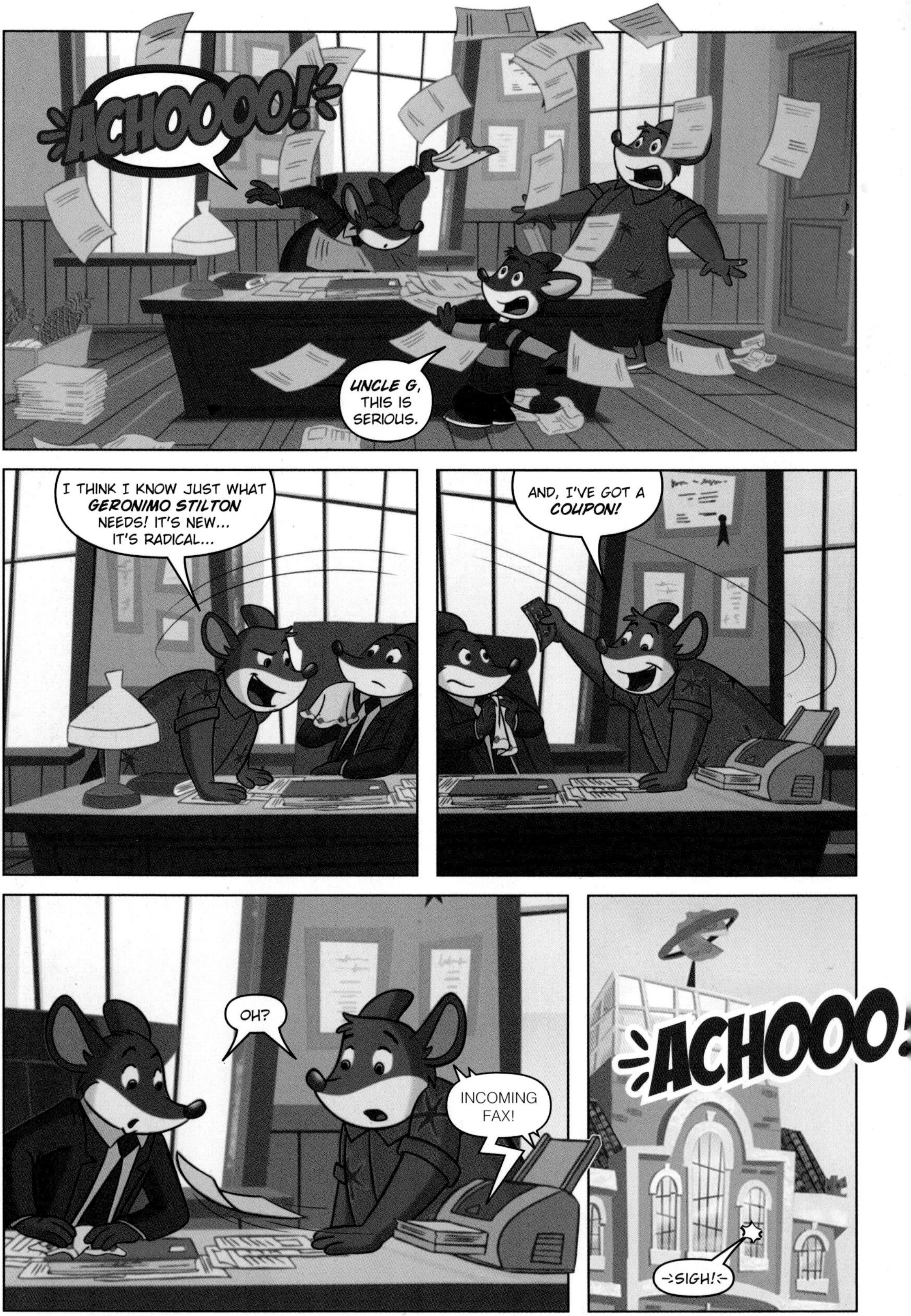
ACHOOOO!
UNCLE G, THIS IS SERIOUS.
I THINK I KNOW JUST WHAT GERONIMO STILTON NEEDS! IT'S NEW... IT'S RADICAL...
AND, I'VE GOT A COUPON!
OH?
INCOMING FAX!
ACHOOO!
SIGH!

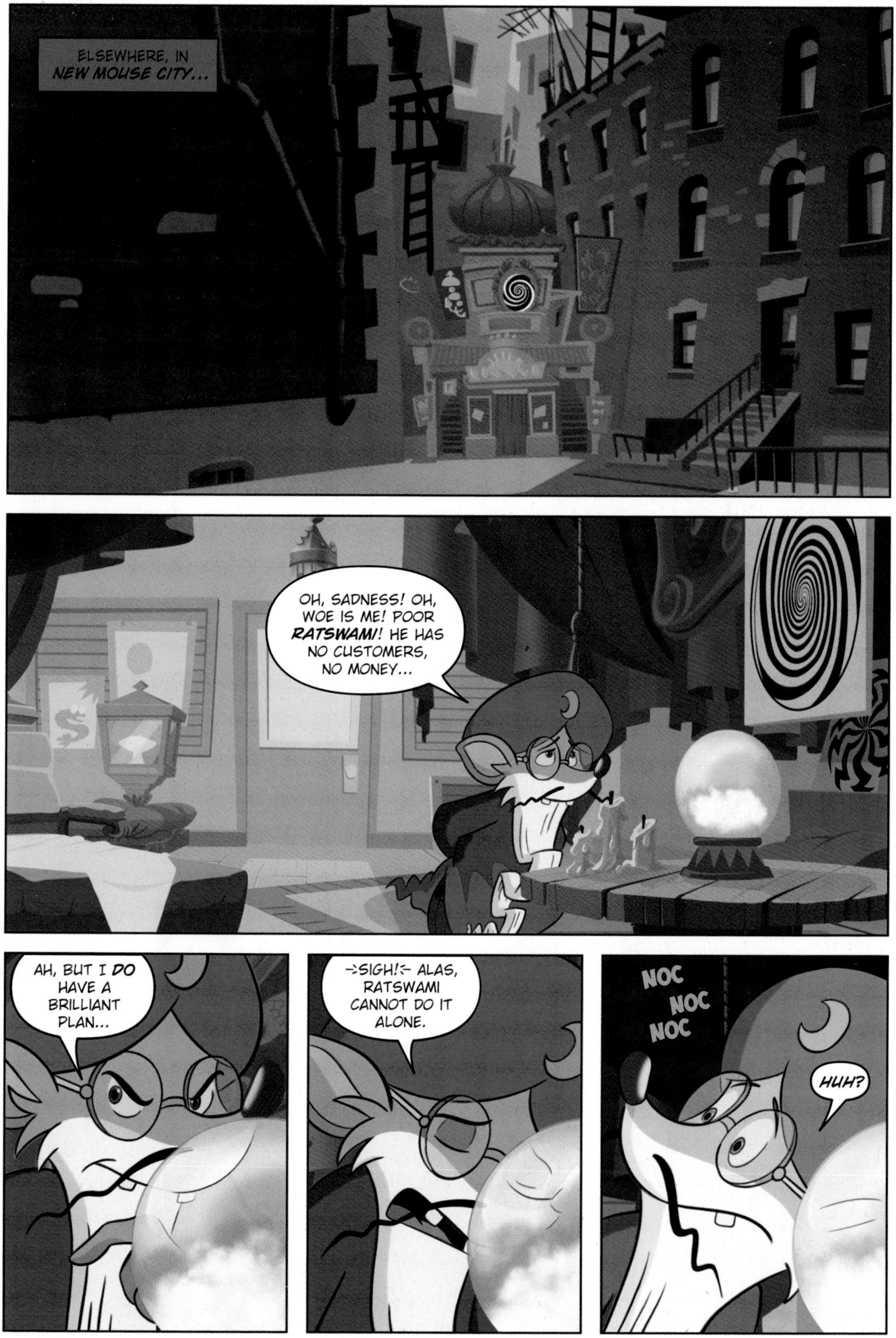
ELSEWHERE, IN NEW MOUSE CITY...
OH, SADNESS! OH, WOE IS ME! POOR RATSWAMI! HE HAS NO CUSTOMERS, NO MONEY...
AH, BUT I DO HAVE A BRILLIANT PLAN...
-SIGH!- ALAS, RATSWAMI CANNOT DO IT ALONE.
NOC NOC NOC
HUH?

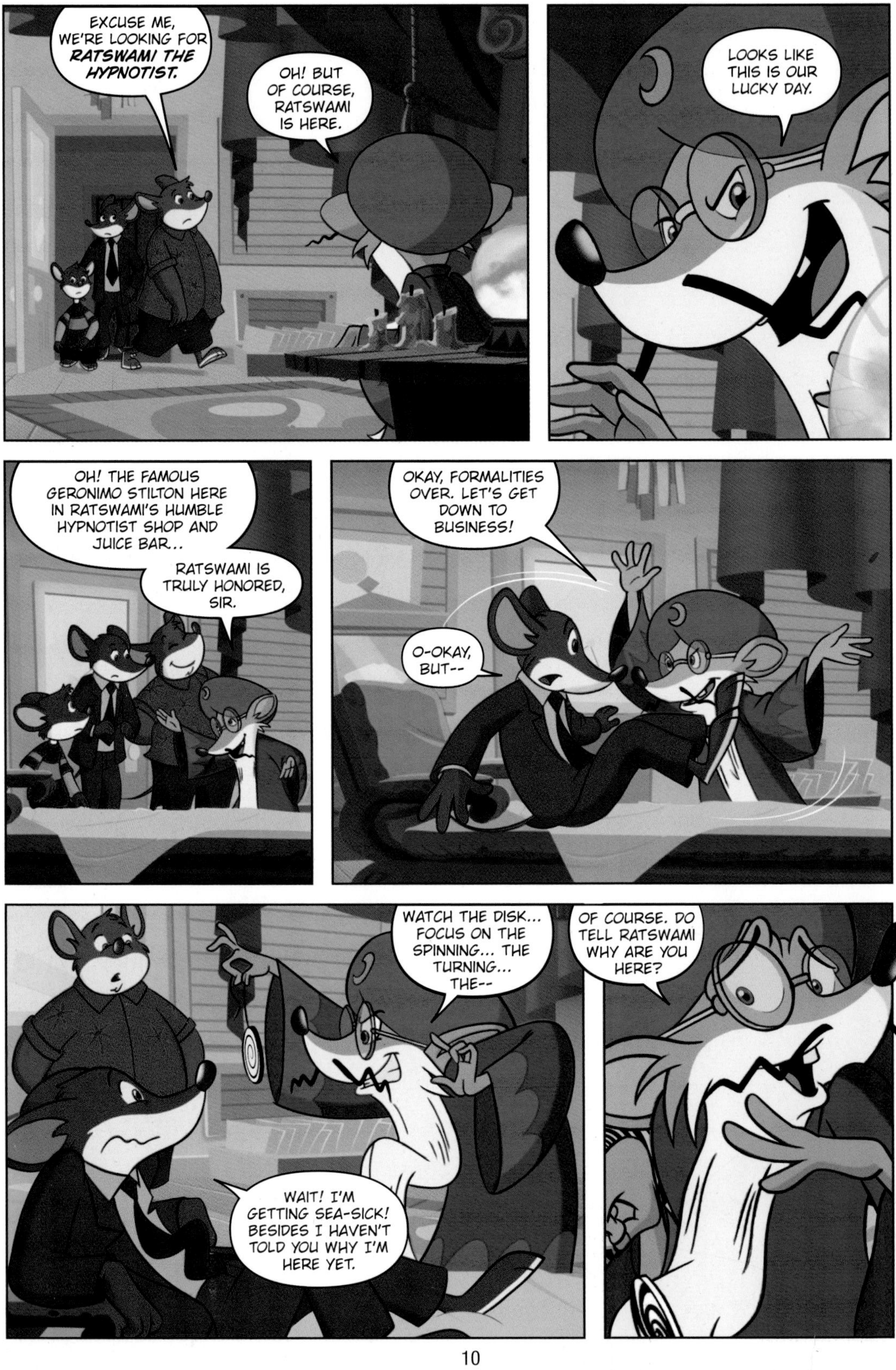
EXCUSE ME, WE'RE LOOKING FOR ***RATSWAMI THE HYPNOTIST.***
OH! BUT OF COURSE, RATSWAMI IS HERE.
LOOKS LIKE THIS IS OUR LUCKY DAY.
OH! THE FAMOUS GERONIMO STILTON HERE IN RATSWAMI'S HUMBLE HYPNOTIST SHOP AND JUICE BAR...
RATSWAMI IS TRULY HONORED, SIR.
OKAY, FORMALITIES OVER. LET'S GET DOWN TO BUSINESS!
O-OKAY, BUT--
WATCH THE DISK... FOCUS ON THE SPINNING... THE TURNING... THE--
WAIT! I'M GETTING SEA-SICK! BESIDES I HAVEN'T TOLD YOU WHY I'M HERE YET.
OF COURSE. DO TELL RATSWAMI WHY ARE YOU HERE?

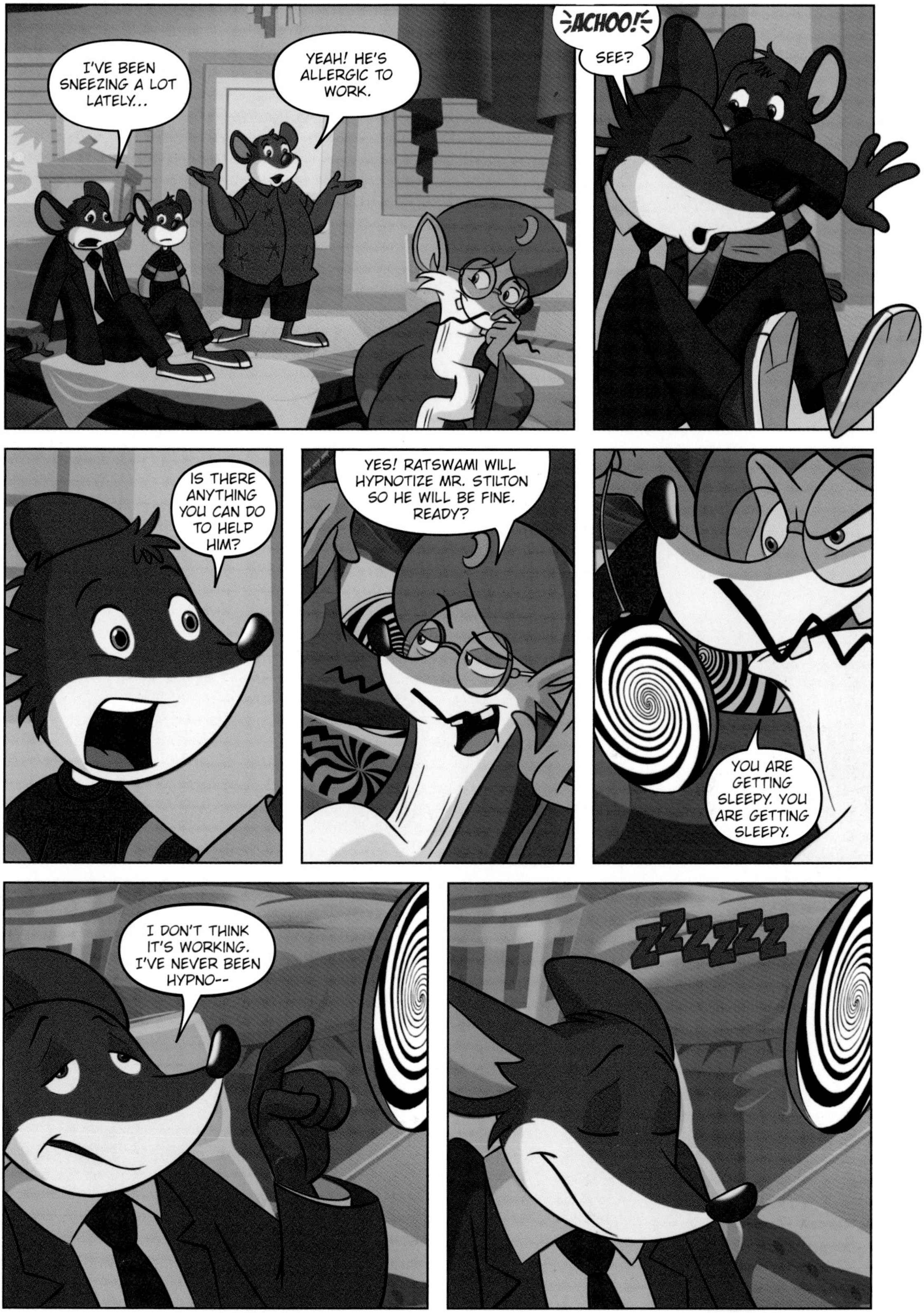
I'VE BEEN SNEEZING A LOT LATELY...
YEAH! HE'S ALLERGIC TO WORK.
ACHOO!
SEE?
IS THERE ANYTHING YOU CAN DO TO HELP HIM?
YES! RATSWAMI WILL HYPNOTIZE MR. STILTON SO HE WILL BE FINE. READY?
YOU ARE GETTING SLEEPY. YOU ARE GETTING SLEEPY.
I DON'T THINK IT'S WORKING. I'VE NEVER BEEN HYPNO--
ZZZZZZ

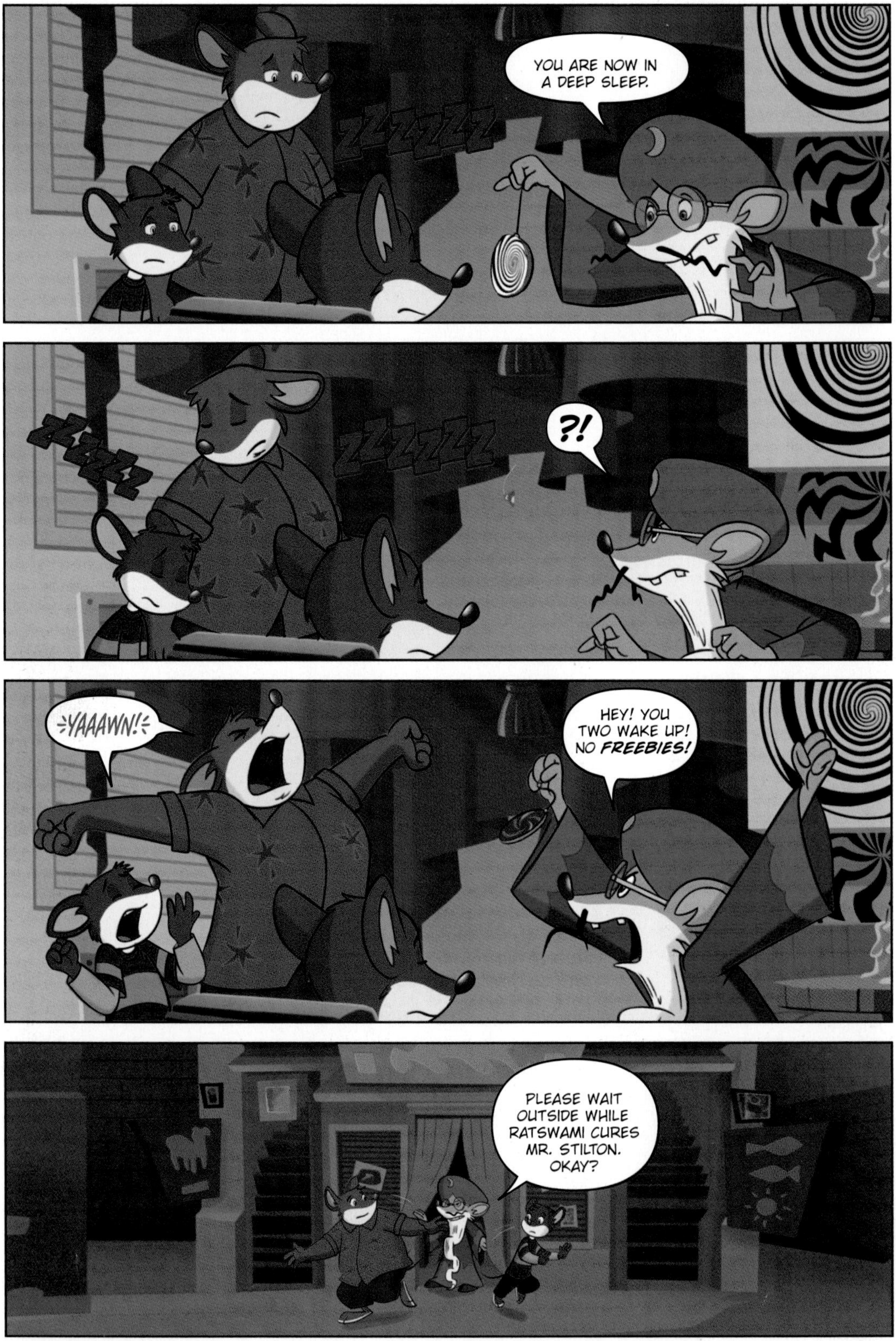
YOU ARE NOW IN A DEEP SLEEP.
?!
YAAAWN!
HEY! YOU TWO WAKE UP! NO *FREEBIES!*
PLEASE WAIT OUTSIDE WHILE RATSWAMI CURES MR. STILTON. OKAY?

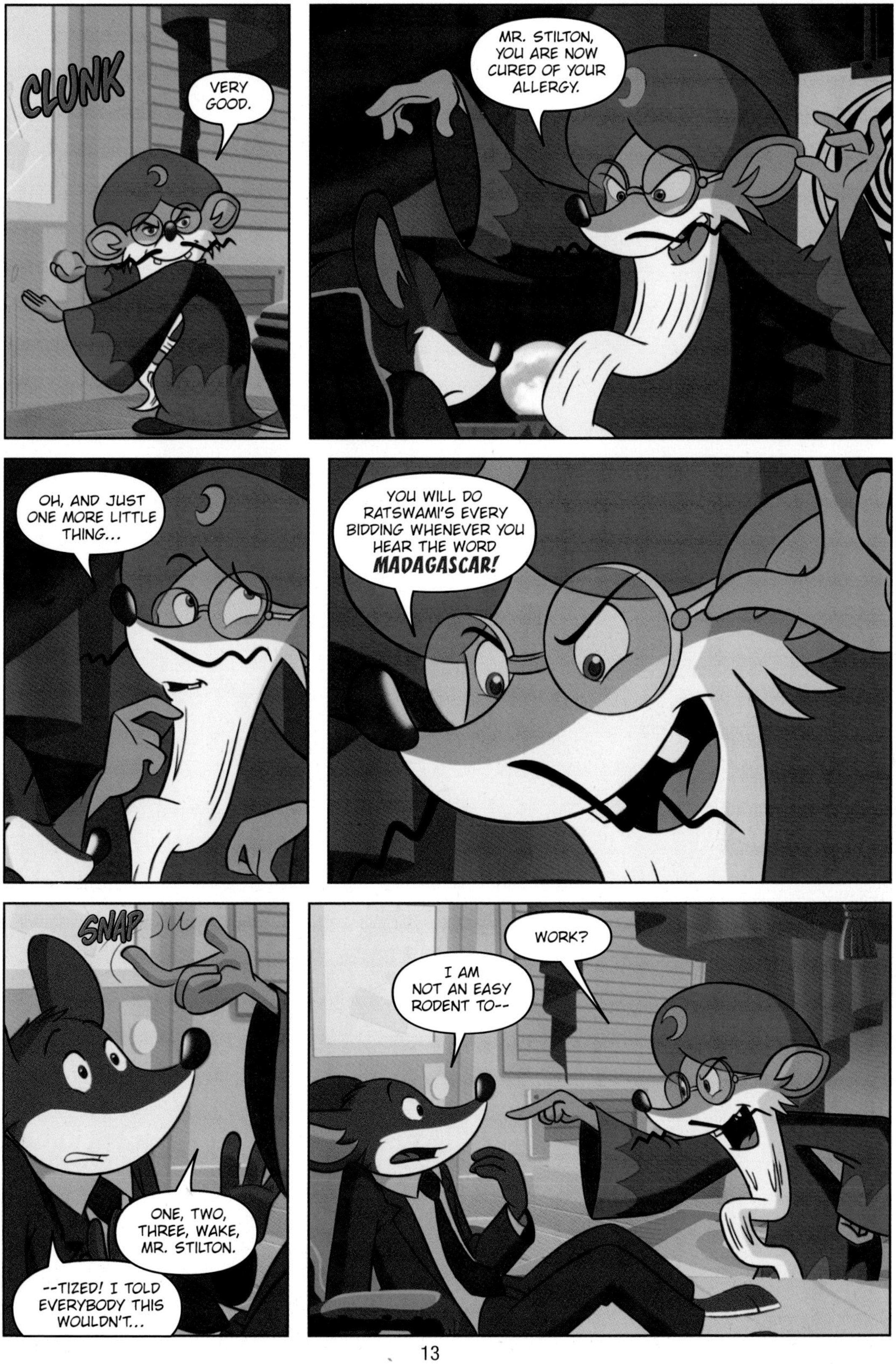
CLUNK
VERY GOOD.
MR. STILTON, YOU ARE NOW CURED OF YOUR ALLERGY.
OH, AND JUST ONE MORE LITTLE THING...
YOU WILL DO RATSWAMI'S EVERY BIDDING WHENEVER YOU HEAR THE WORD MADAGASCAR!
SNAP
ONE, TWO, THREE, WAKE, MR. STILTON.
--TIZED! I TOLD EVERYBODY THIS WOULDN'T...
WORK?
I AM NOT AN EASY RODENT TO--

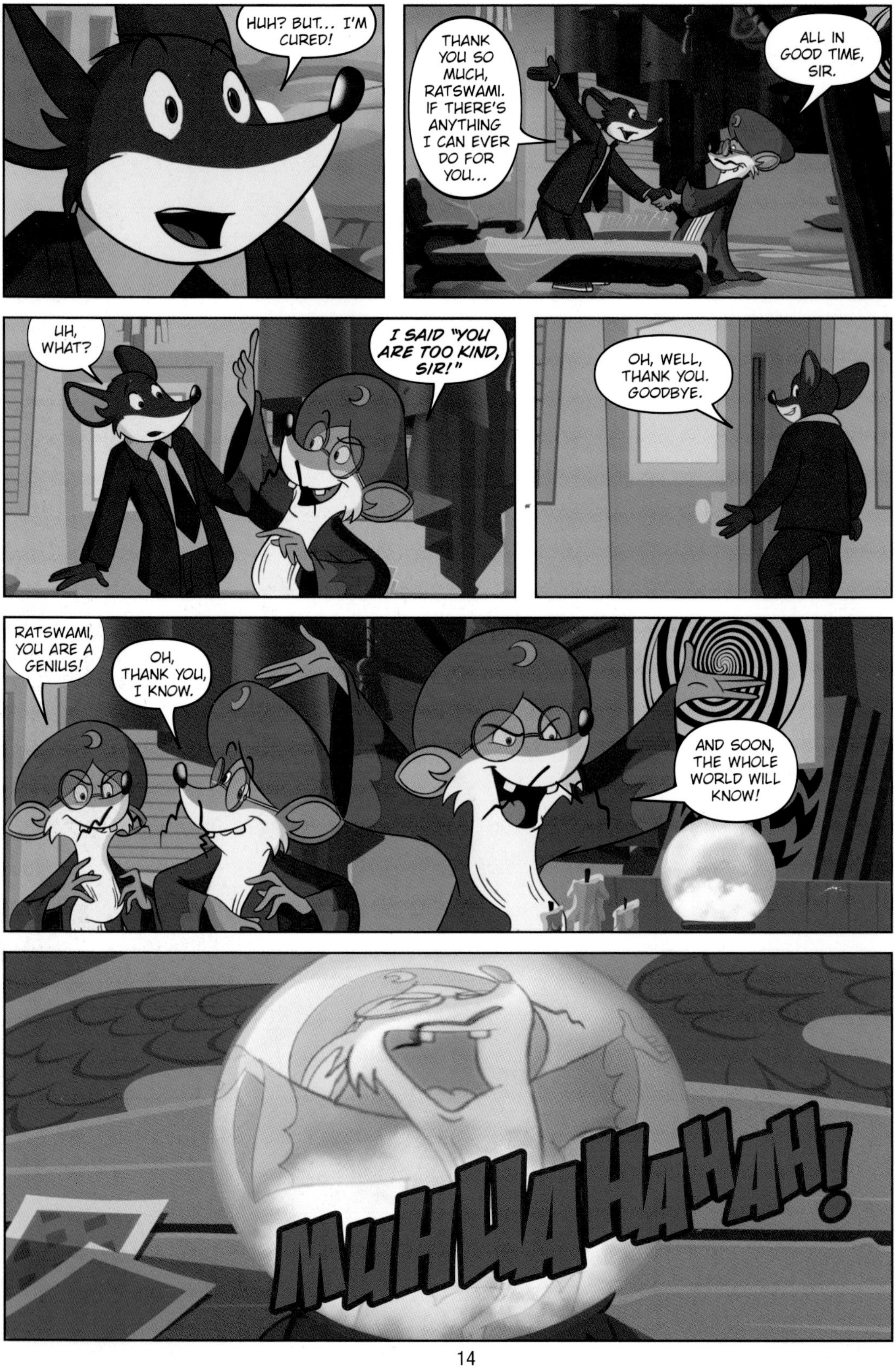

HUH? BUT... I'M CURED!
THANK YOU SO MUCH, RATSWAMI. IF THERE'S ANYTHING I CAN EVER DO FOR YOU...
ALL IN GOOD TIME, SIR.
UH, WHAT?
I SAID "YOU ARE TOO KIND, SIR!"
OH, WELL, THANK YOU. GOODBYE.
RATSWAMI, YOU ARE A GENIUS!
OH, THANK YOU, I KNOW.
AND SOON, THE WHOLE WORLD WILL KNOW!
MUHUAHAHAH!

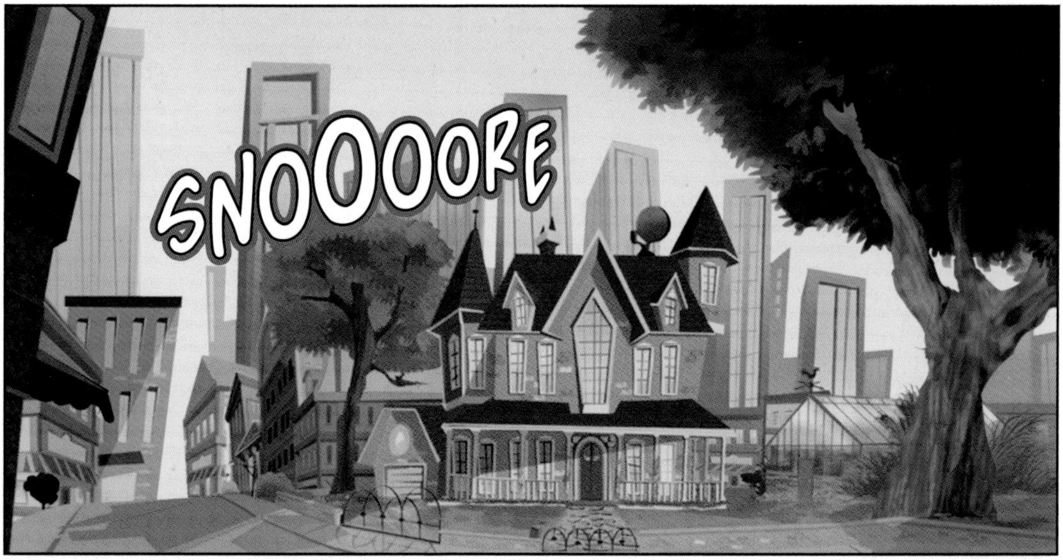
SNOOOORE

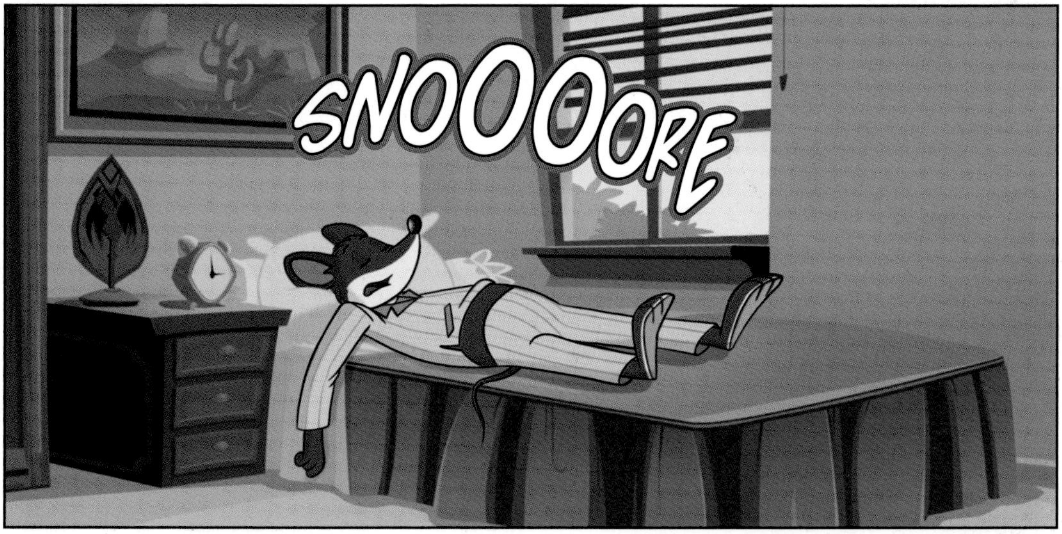
SNOOOORE

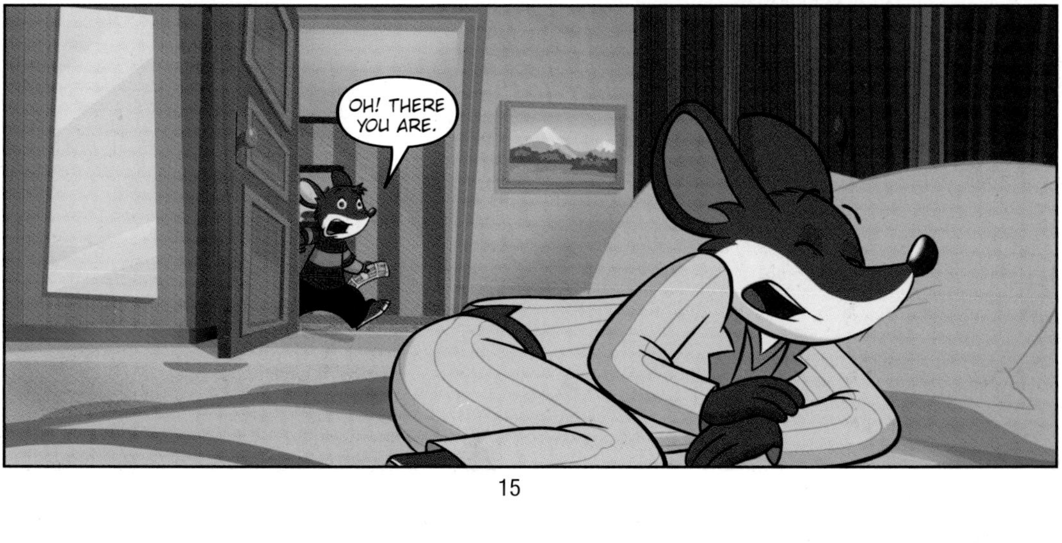
OH! THERE YOU ARE.

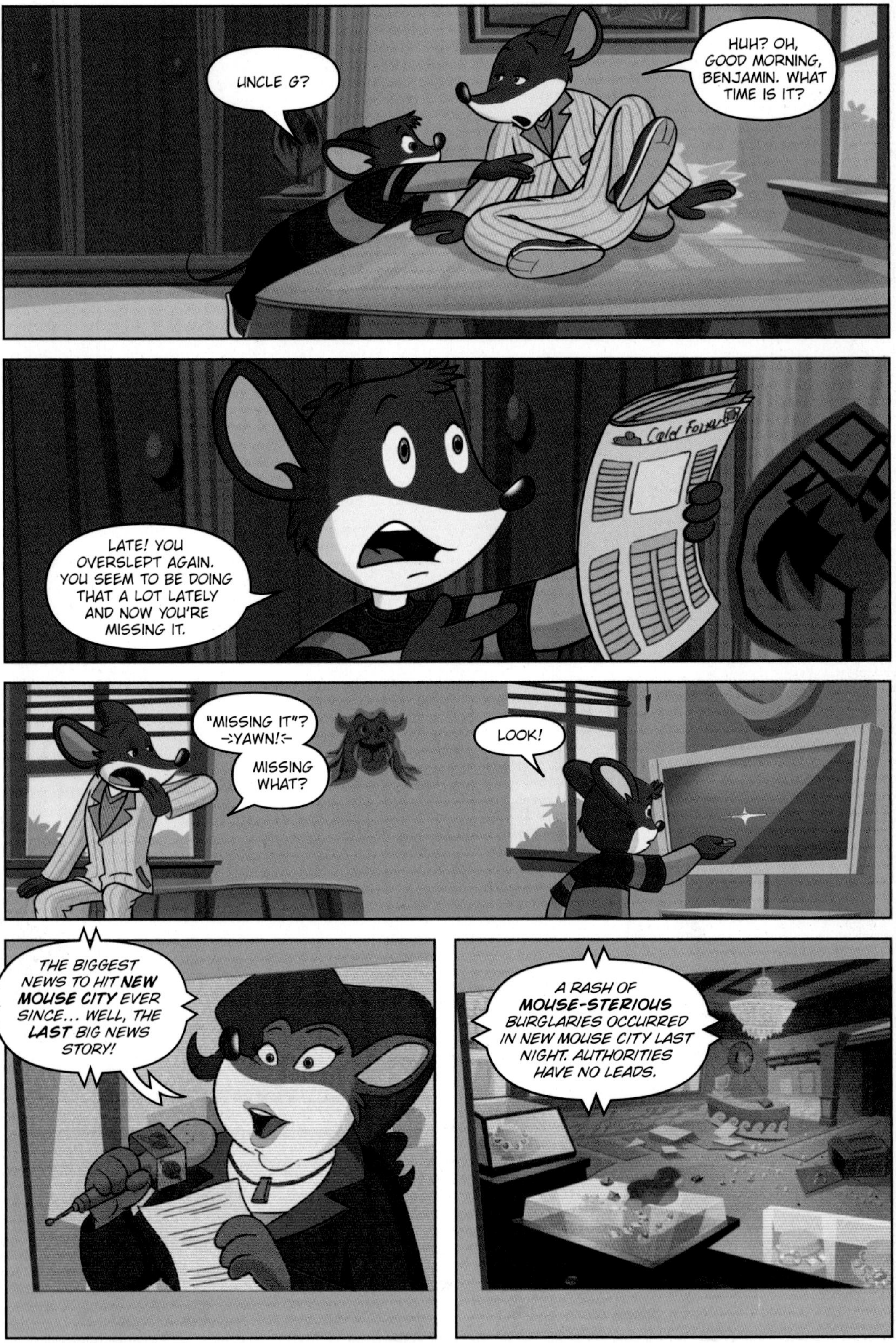
UNCLE G?
HUH? OH, GOOD MORNING, BENJAMIN. WHAT TIME IS IT?
LATE! YOU OVERSLEPT AGAIN. YOU SEEM TO BE DOING THAT A LOT LATELY AND NOW YOU'RE MISSING IT.
"MISSING IT"? ~YAWN!~
MISSING WHAT?
LOOK!
THE BIGGEST NEWS TO HIT NEW MOUSE CITY EVER SINCE... WELL, THE LAST BIG NEWS STORY!
A RASH OF MOUSE-STERIOUS BURGLARIES OCCURRED IN NEW MOUSE CITY LAST NIGHT. AUTHORITIES HAVE NO LEADS.

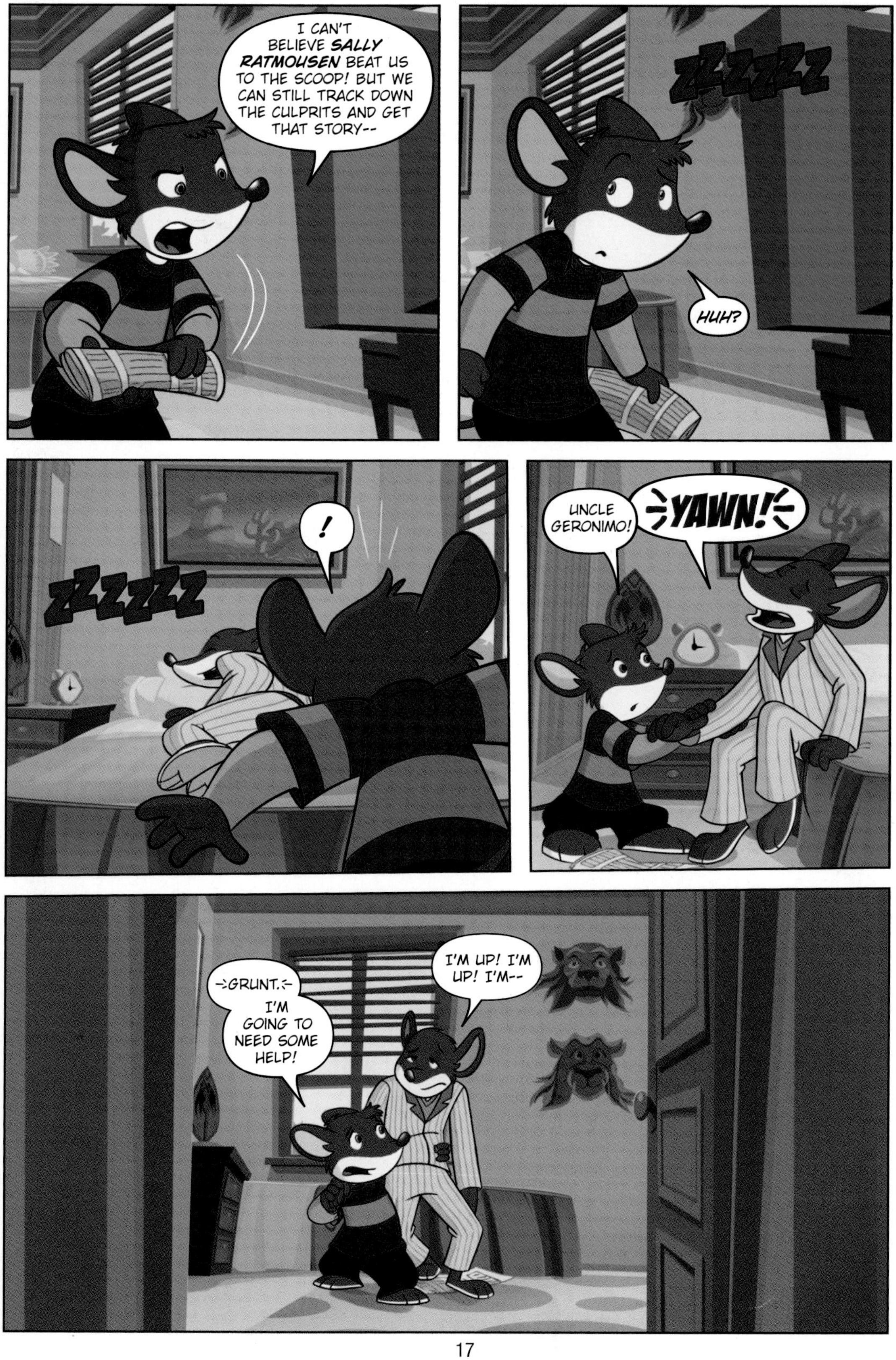
I CAN'T BELIEVE **SALLY RATMOUSEN** BEAT US TO THE SCOOP! BUT WE CAN STILL TRACK DOWN THE CULPRITS AND GET THAT STORY--
ZZZZZZ
HUH?
ZZZZZZ
!
UNCLE GERONIMO!
YAWN!
GRUNT.
I'M GOING TO NEED SOME HELP!
I'M UP! I'M UP! I'M--

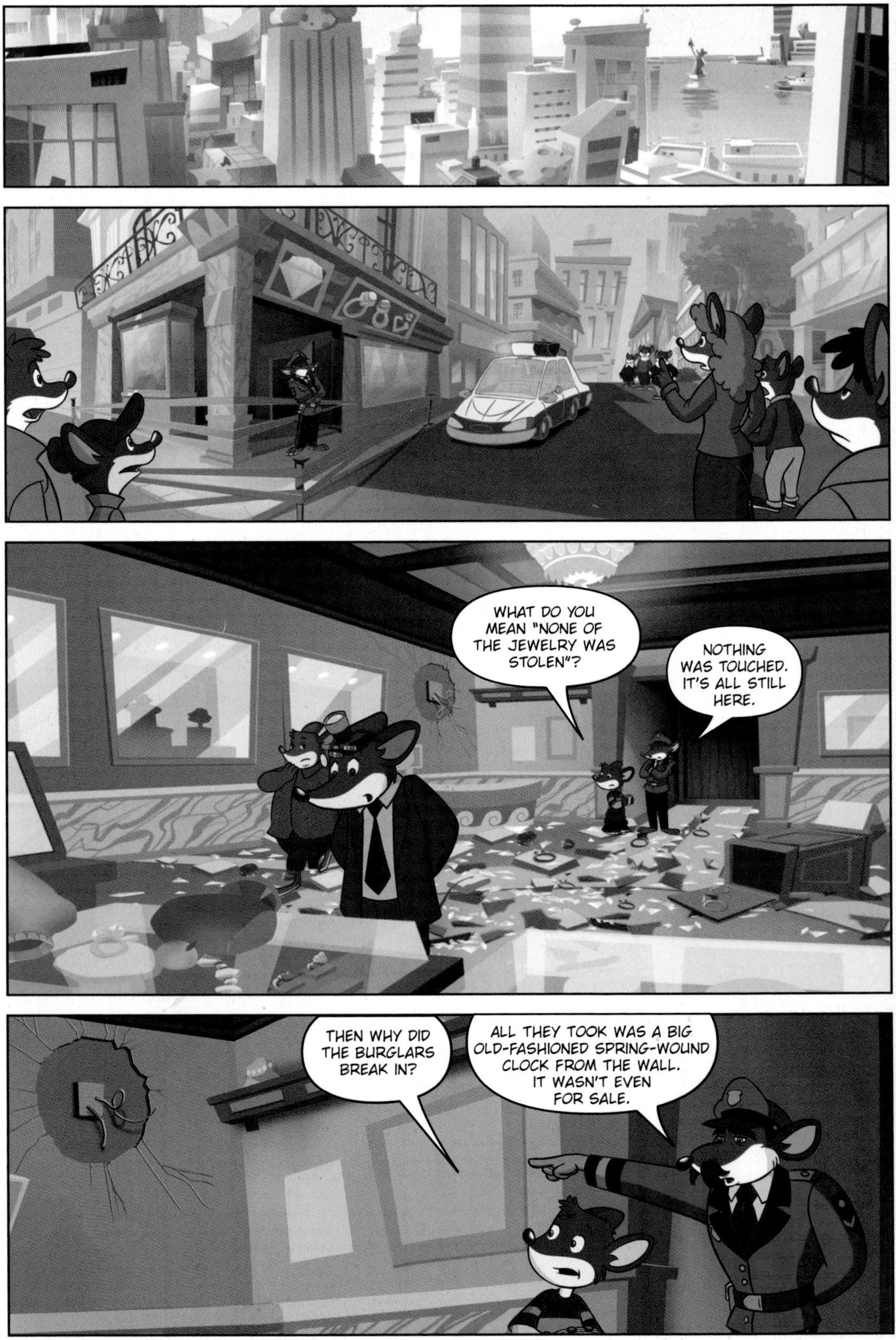
WHAT DO YOU MEAN "NONE OF THE JEWELRY WAS STOLEN"?
NOTHING WAS TOUCHED. IT'S ALL STILL HERE.
THEN WHY DID THE BURGLARS BREAK IN?
ALL THEY TOOK WAS A BIG OLD-FASHIONED SPRING-WOUND CLOCK FROM THE WALL. IT WASN'T EVEN FOR SALE.

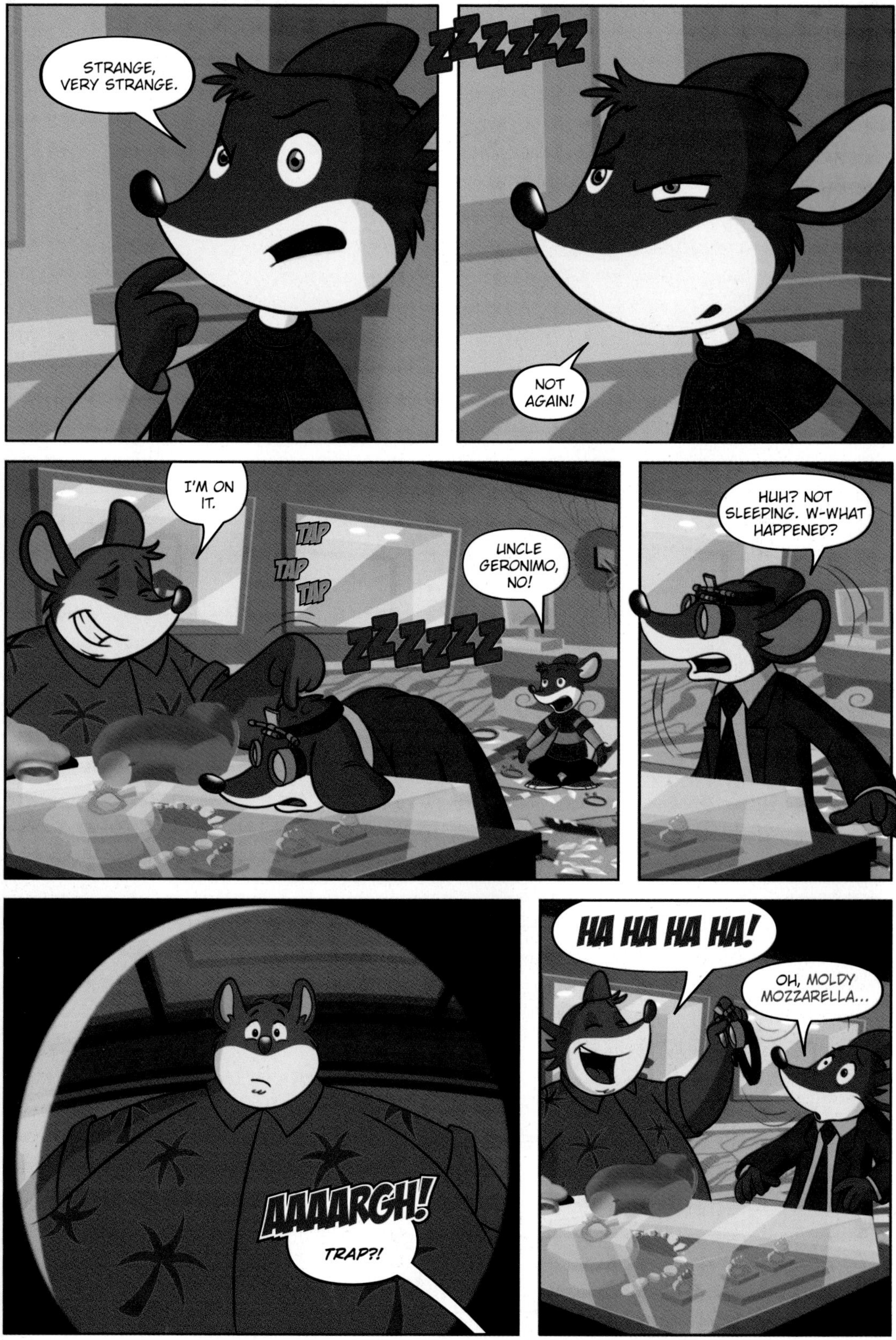

STRANGE, VERY STRANGE.
ZZZZZZ
NOT AGAIN!
I'M ON IT.
TAP
TAP
TAP
ZZZZZZ
UNCLE GERONIMO, NO!
HUH? NOT SLEEPING. W-WHAT HAPPENED?
AAAARGH!
TRAP?!
HA HA HA HA!
OH, MOLDY MOZZARELLA...

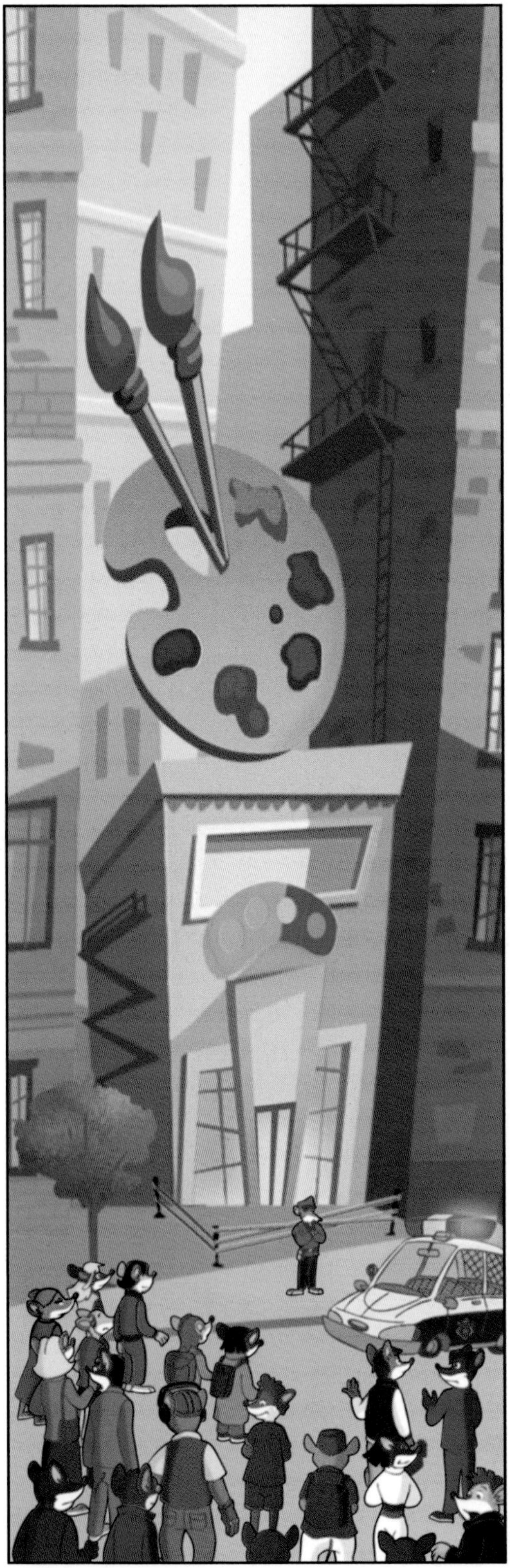

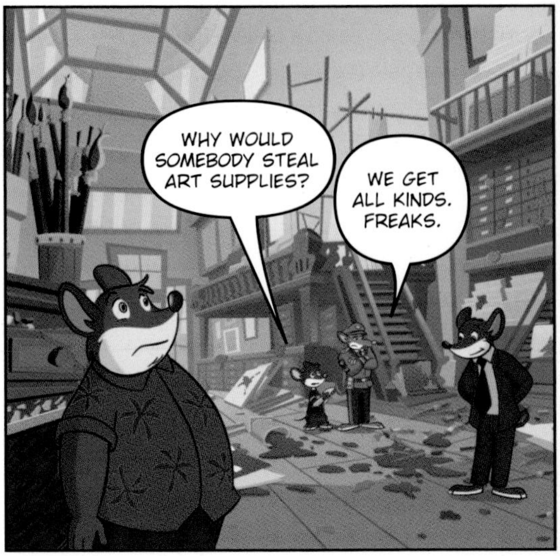
WHY WOULD SOMEBODY STEAL ART SUPPLIES?
WE GET ALL KINDS. FREAKS.

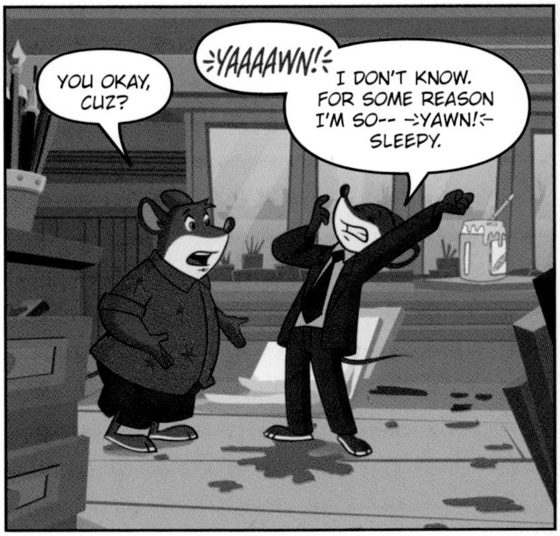
YOU OKAY, CUZ?
-YAAAAWN!- I DON'T KNOW. FOR SOME REASON I'M SO-- -YAWN!- SLEEPY.

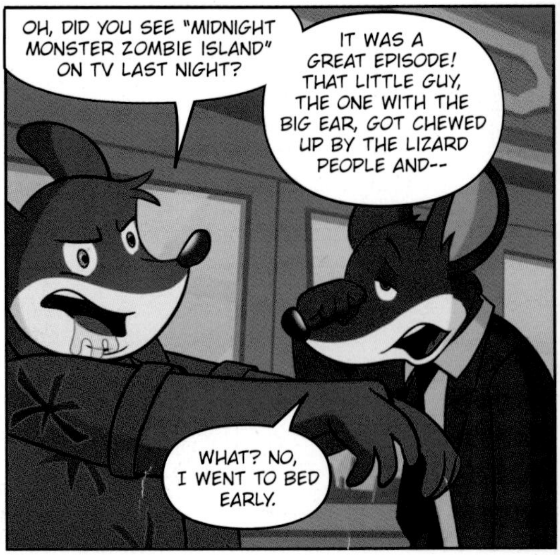
OH, DID YOU SEE "MIDNIGHT MONSTER ZOMBIE ISLAND" ON TV LAST NIGHT?
IT WAS A GREAT EPISODE! THAT LITTLE GUY, THE ONE WITH THE BIG EAR, GOT CHEWED UP BY THE LIZARD PEOPLE AND--
WHAT? NO, I WENT TO BED EARLY.

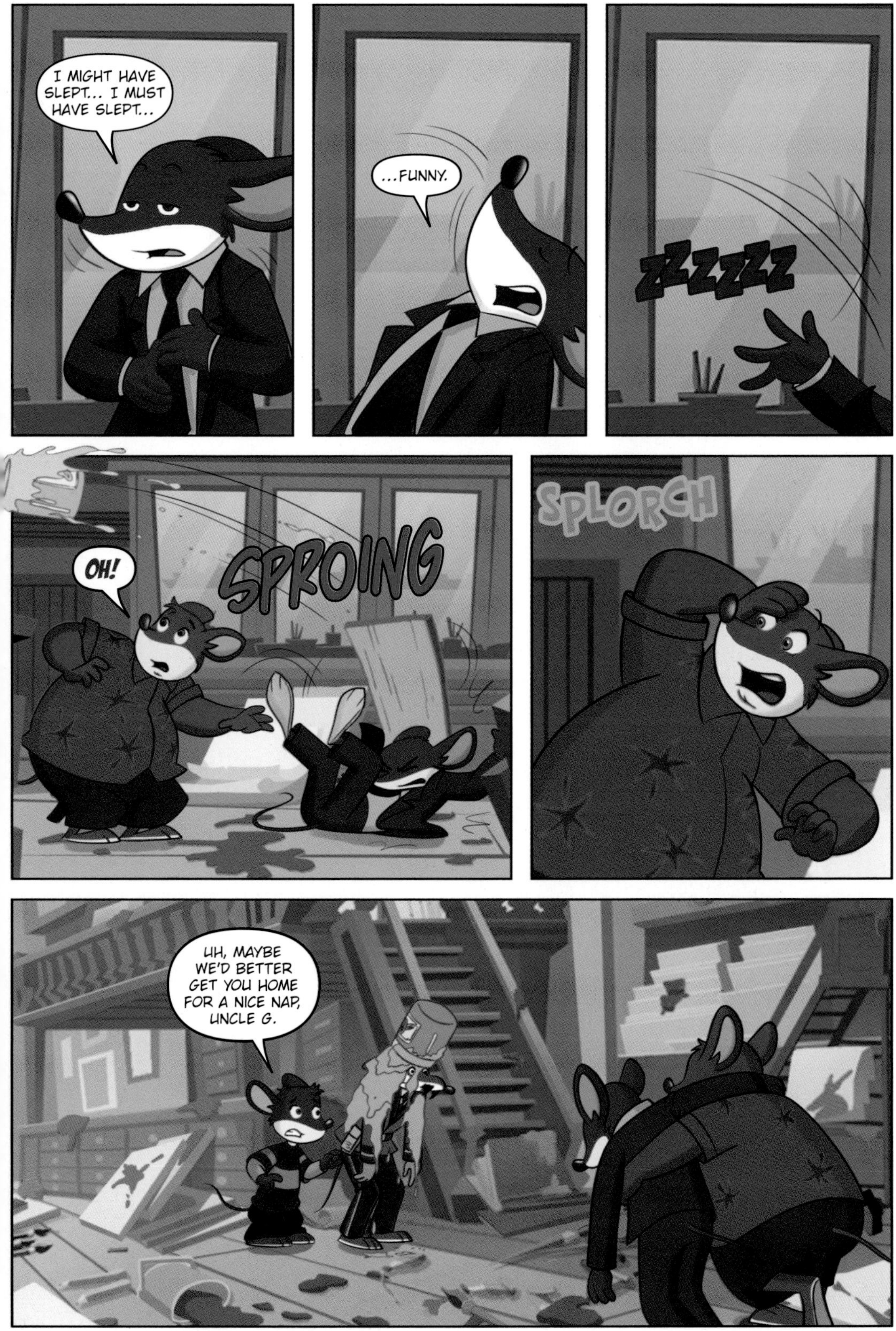
I MIGHT HAVE SLEPT... I MUST HAVE SLEPT...
...FUNNY.
ZZZZZZ
OH!
SPROING
SPLORCH
UH, MAYBE WE'D BETTER GET YOU HOME FOR A NICE NAP, UNCLE G.

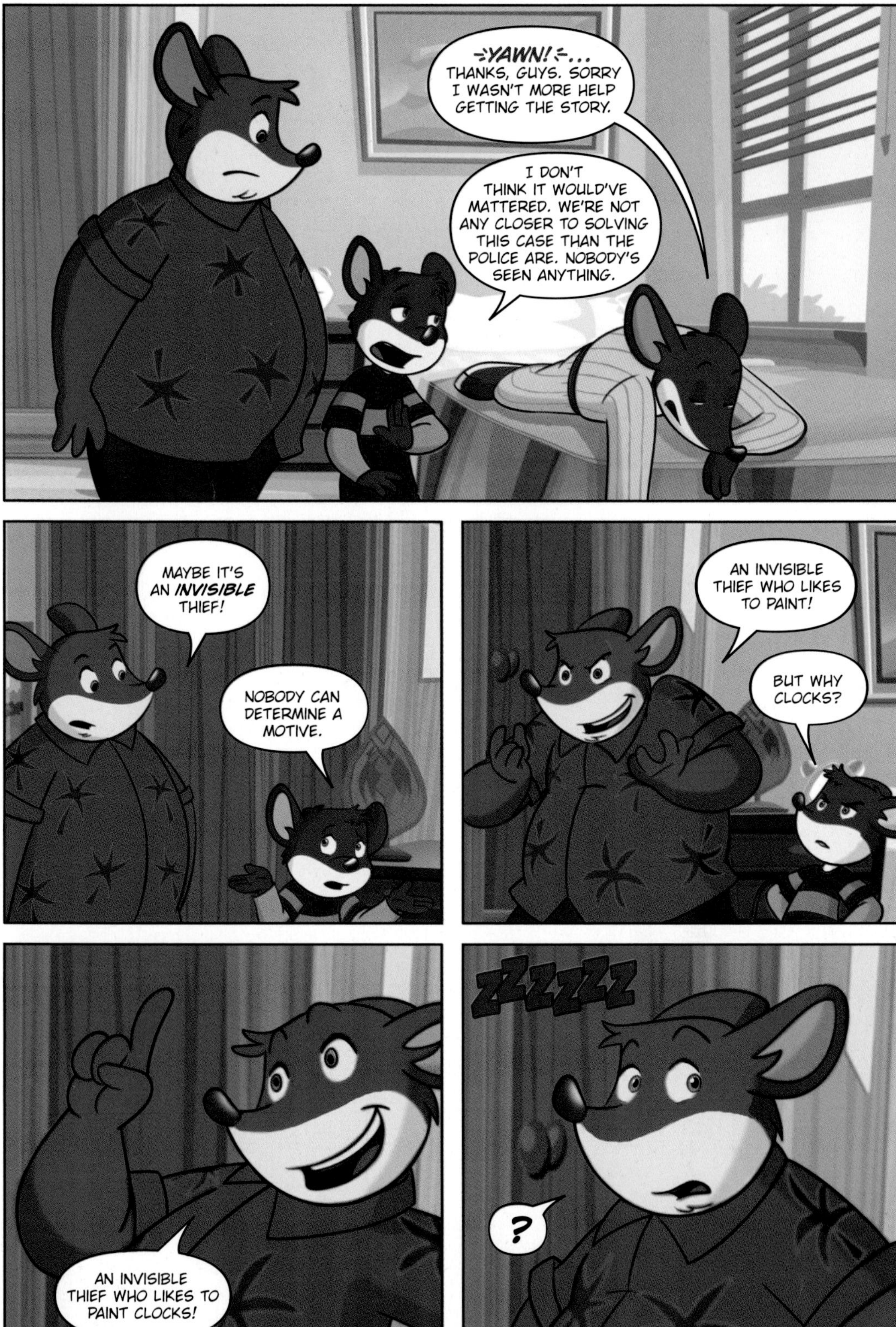
YAWN!...
THANKS, GUYS. SORRY I WASN'T MORE HELP GETTING THE STORY.
I DON'T THINK IT WOULD'VE MATTERED. WE'RE NOT ANY CLOSER TO SOLVING THIS CASE THAN THE POLICE ARE. NOBODY'S SEEN ANYTHING.
MAYBE IT'S AN *INVISIBLE* THIEF!
NOBODY CAN DETERMINE A MOTIVE.
AN INVISIBLE THIEF WHO LIKES TO PAINT!
BUT WHY CLOCKS?
AN INVISIBLE THIEF WHO LIKES TO PAINT CLOCKS!
ZZZZZZ
?

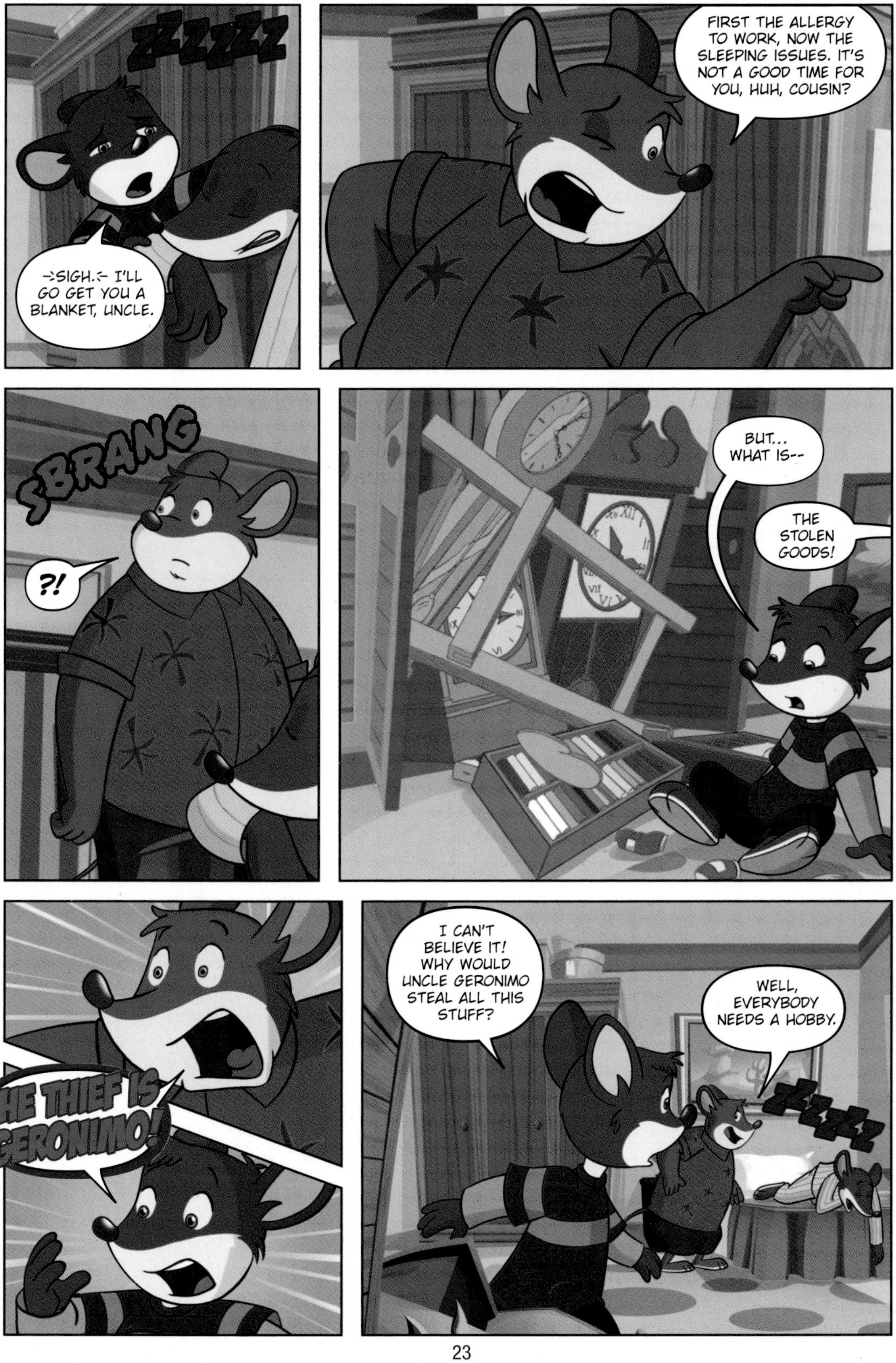
ZZZZZZ
⇒SIGH.⇐ I'LL GO GET YOU A BLANKET, UNCLE.
FIRST THE ALLERGY TO WORK, NOW THE SLEEPING ISSUES. IT'S NOT A GOOD TIME FOR YOU, HUH, COUSIN?
SBRANG
?!
BUT... WHAT IS--
THE STOLEN GOODS!
THE THIEF IS GERONIMO!
I CAN'T BELIEVE IT! WHY WOULD UNCLE GERONIMO STEAL ALL THIS STUFF?
WELL, EVERYBODY NEEDS A HOBBY.
ZZZZZ

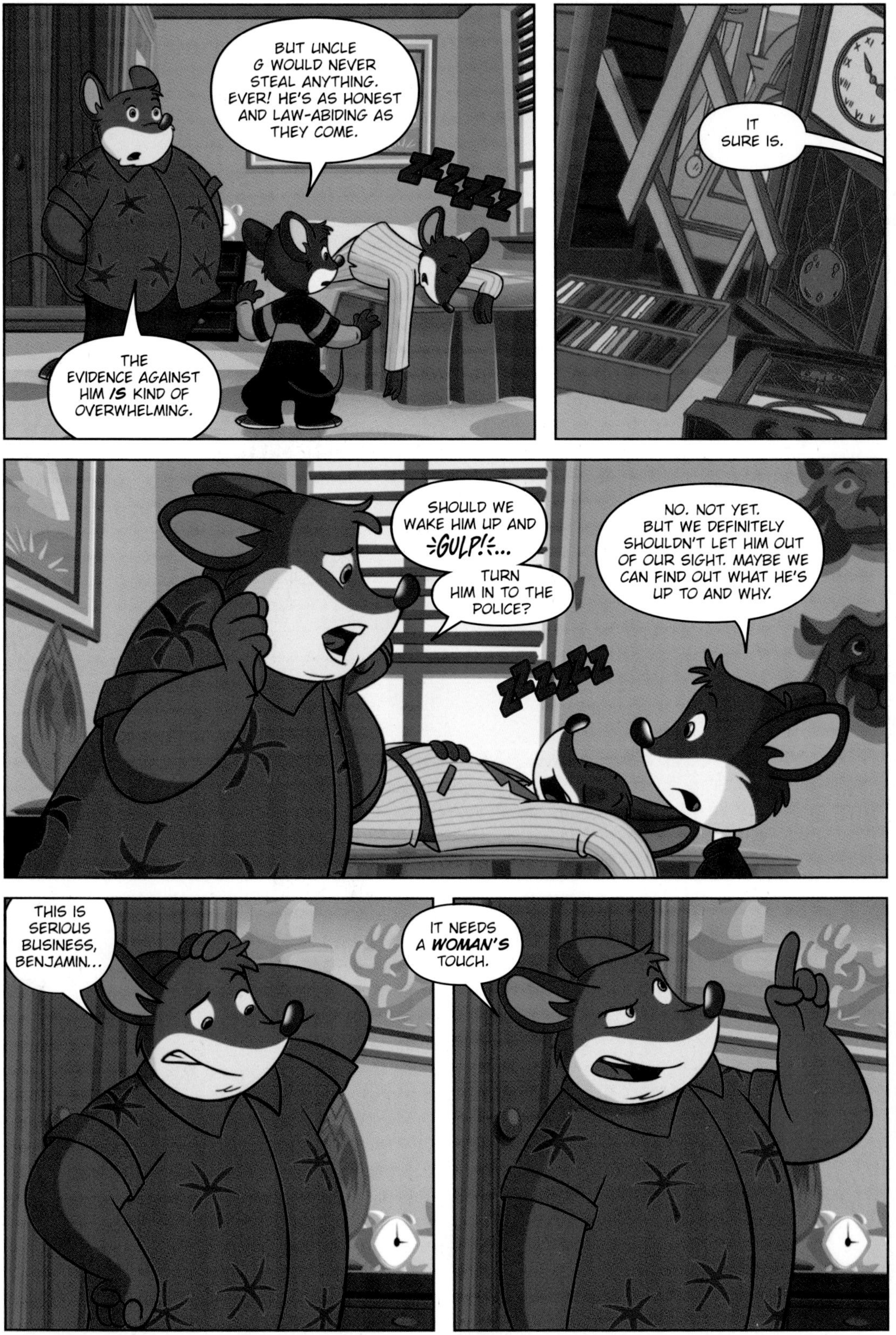

BUT UNCLE G WOULD NEVER STEAL ANYTHING. EVER! HE'S AS HONEST AND LAW-ABIDING AS THEY COME.
ZZZZZ
THE EVIDENCE AGAINST HIM IS KIND OF OVERWHELMING.
IT SURE IS.
SHOULD WE WAKE HIM UP AND GULP!... TURN HIM IN TO THE POLICE?
NO. NOT YET. BUT WE DEFINITELY SHOULDN'T LET HIM OUT OF OUR SIGHT. MAYBE WE CAN FIND OUT WHAT HE'S UP TO AND WHY.
ZZZZZ
THIS IS SERIOUS BUSINESS, BENJAMIN...
IT NEEDS A WOMAN'S TOUCH.

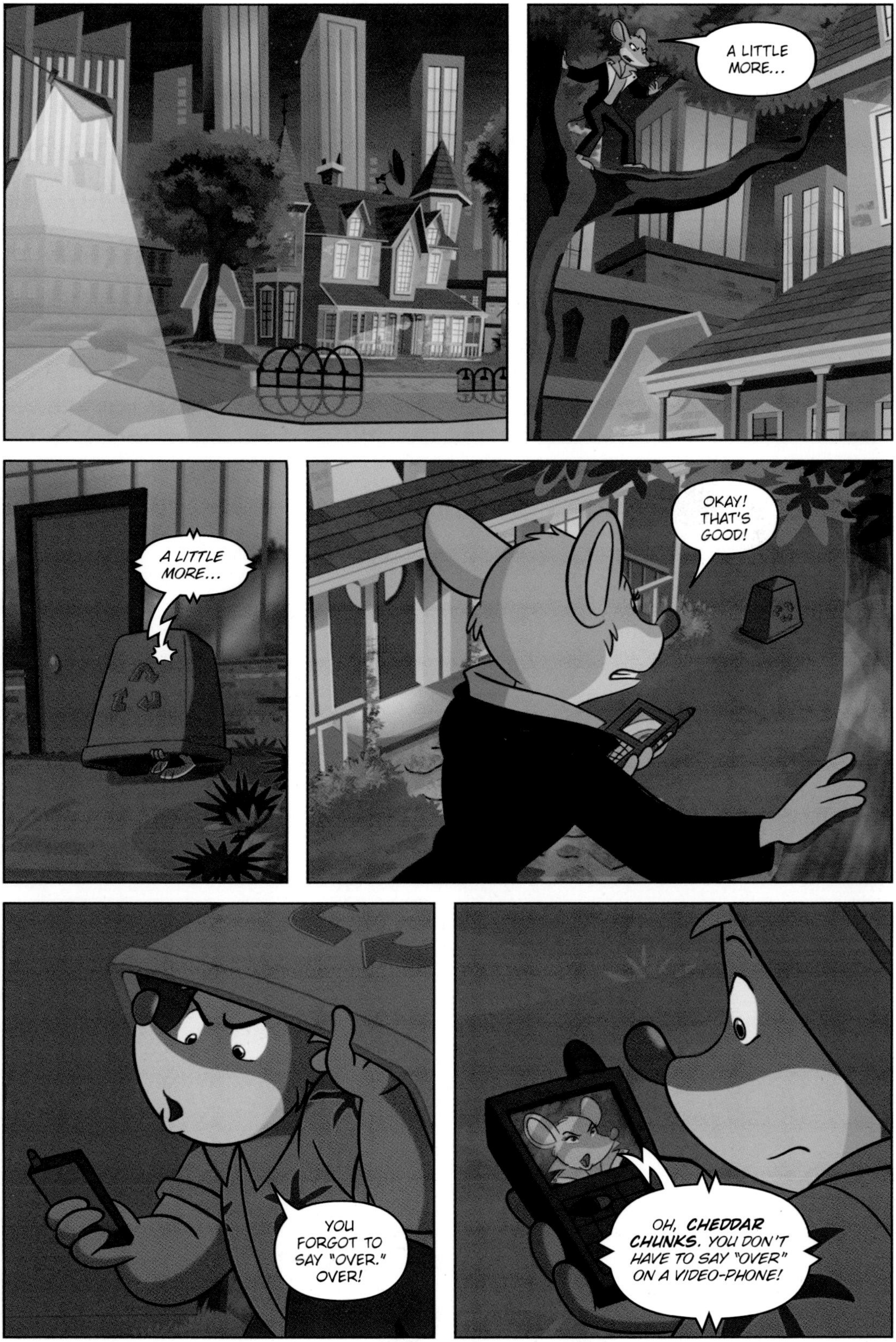
A LITTLE MORE...
A LITTLE MORE...
OKAY! THAT'S GOOD!
YOU FORGOT TO SAY "OVER." OVER!
OH, **CHEDDAR CHUNKS**. YOU DON'T HAVE TO SAY "OVER" ON A VIDEO-PHONE!

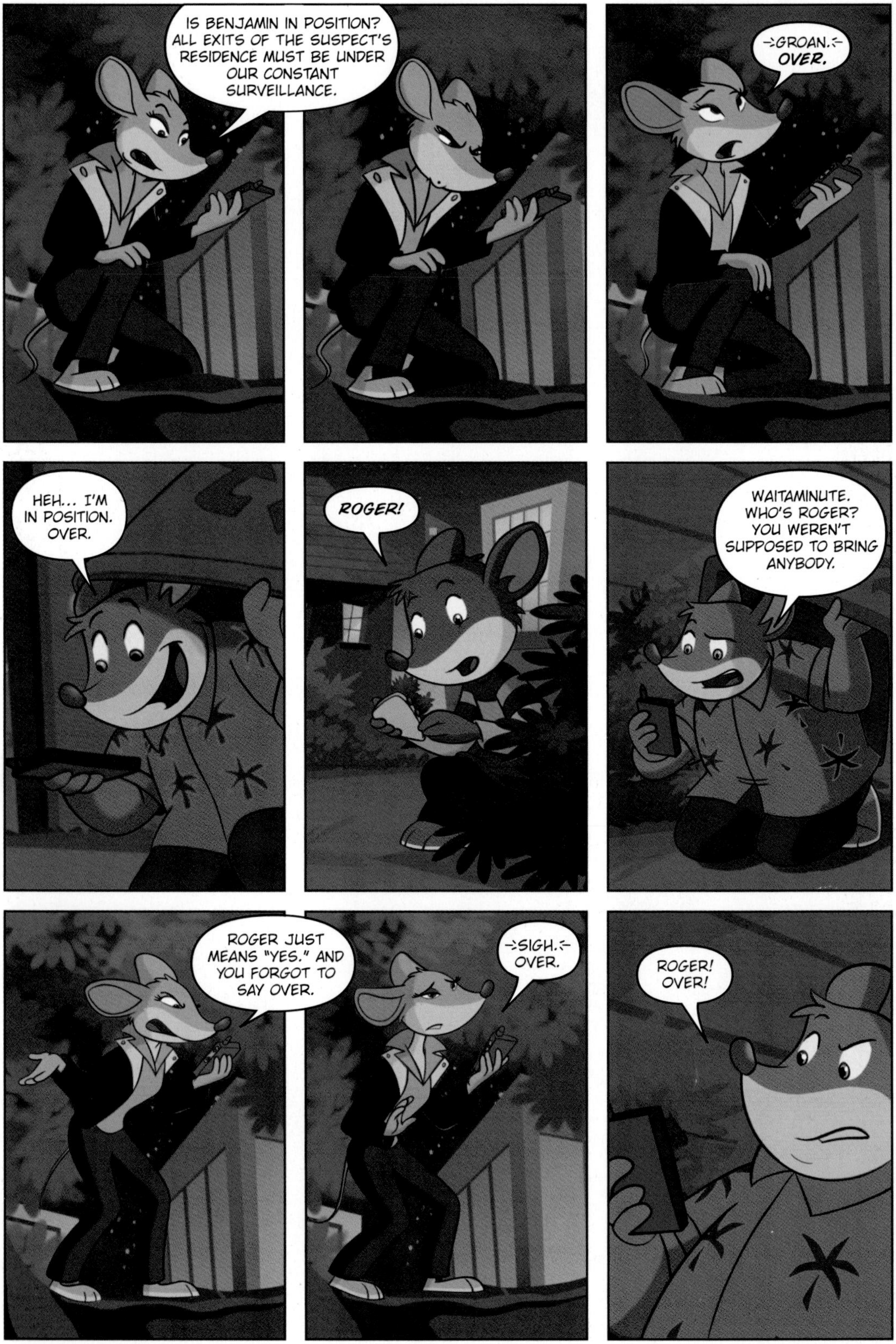
IS BENJAMIN IN POSITION? ALL EXITS OF THE SUSPECT'S RESIDENCE MUST BE UNDER OUR CONSTANT SURVEILLANCE.
-GROAN.- **OVER.**
HEH... I'M IN POSITION. OVER.
***ROGER!***
WAITAMINUTE. WHO'S ROGER? YOU WEREN'T SUPPOSED TO BRING ANYBODY.
ROGER JUST MEANS "YES." AND YOU FORGOT TO SAY OVER.
-SIGH.- OVER.
ROGER! OVER!

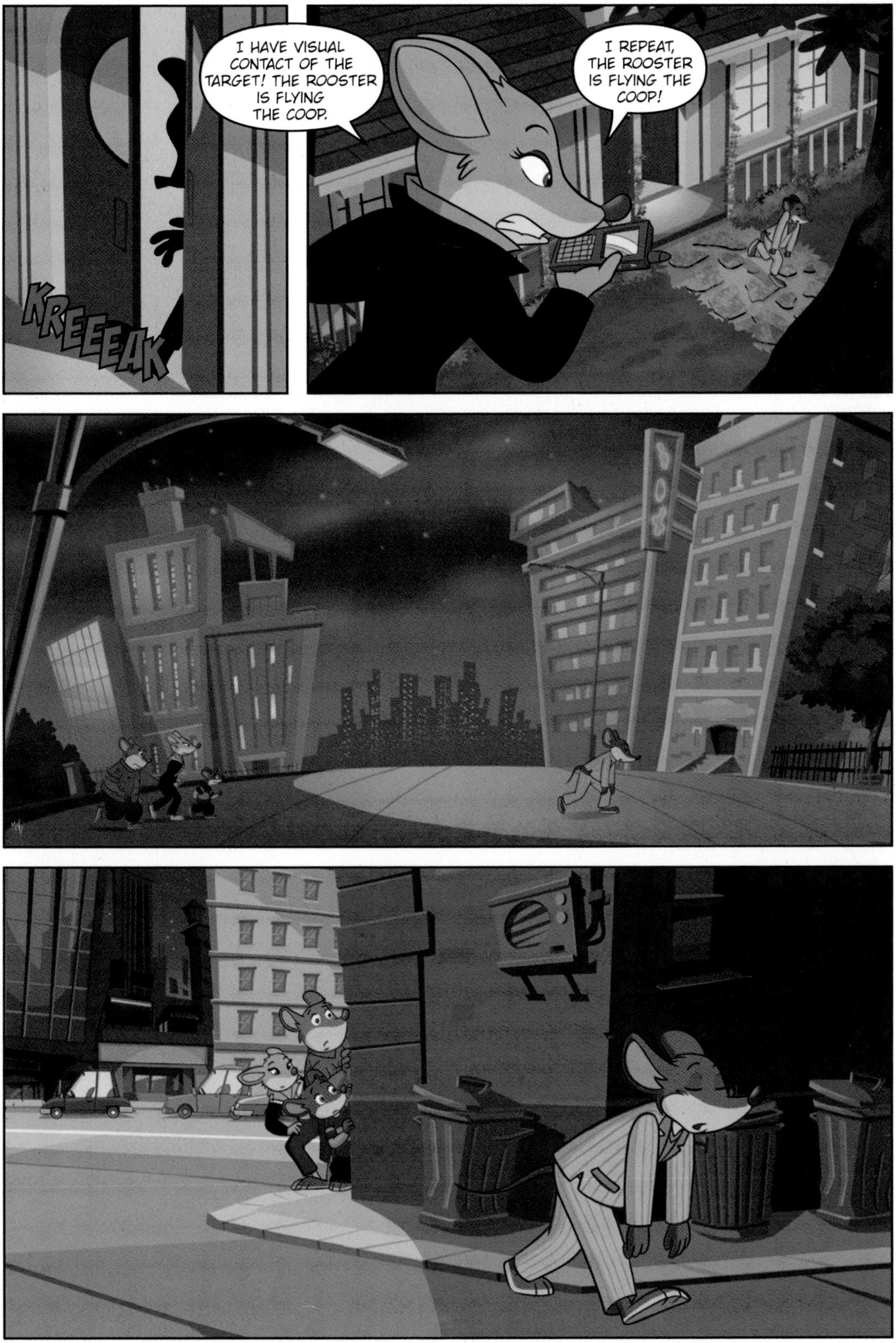
KREEEAK
I HAVE VISUAL CONTACT OF THE TARGET! THE ROOSTER IS FLYING THE COOP.
I REPEAT, THE ROOSTER IS FLYING THE COOP!

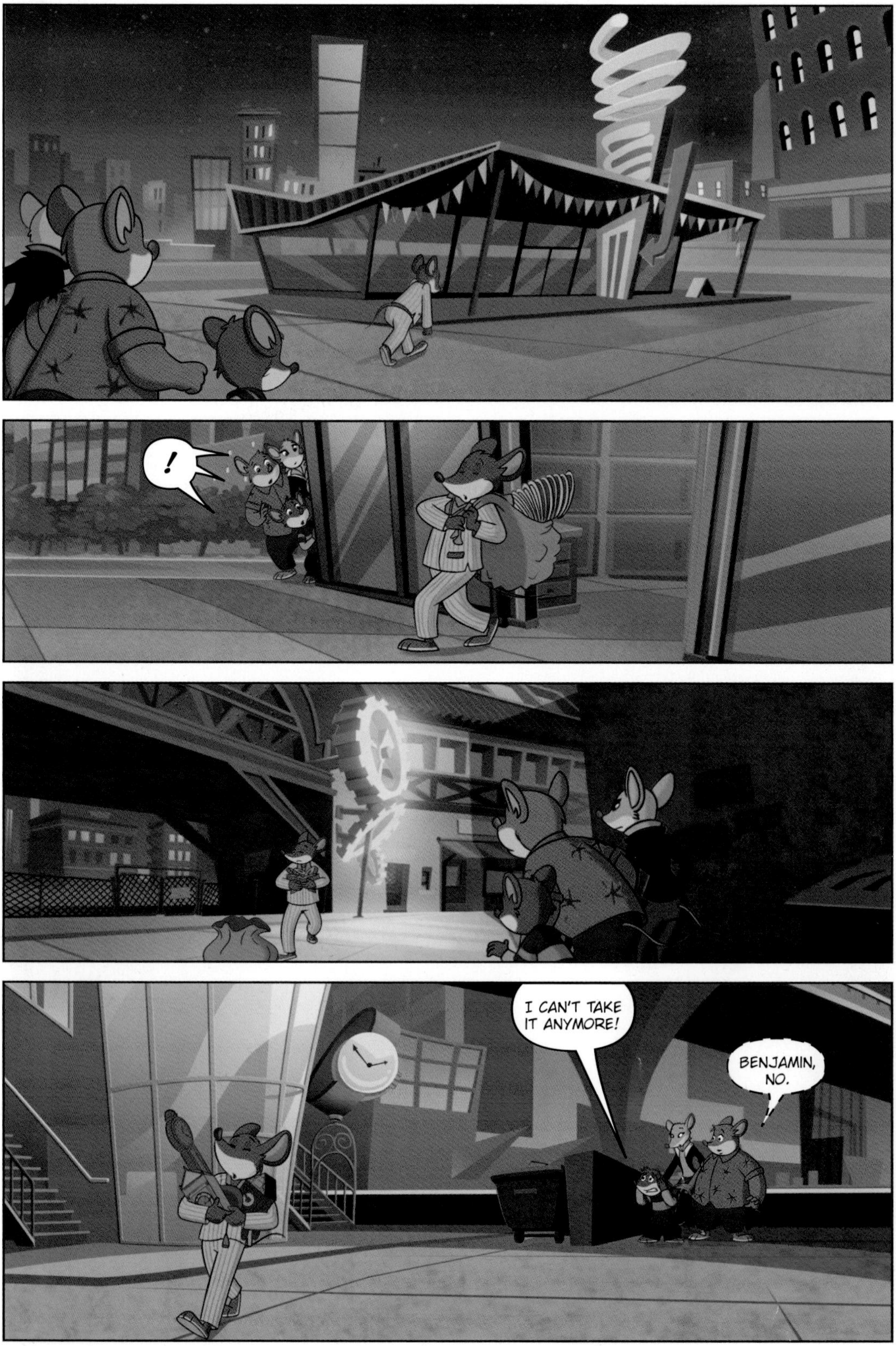
!
I CAN'T TAKE IT ANYMORE!
BENJAMIN, NO.

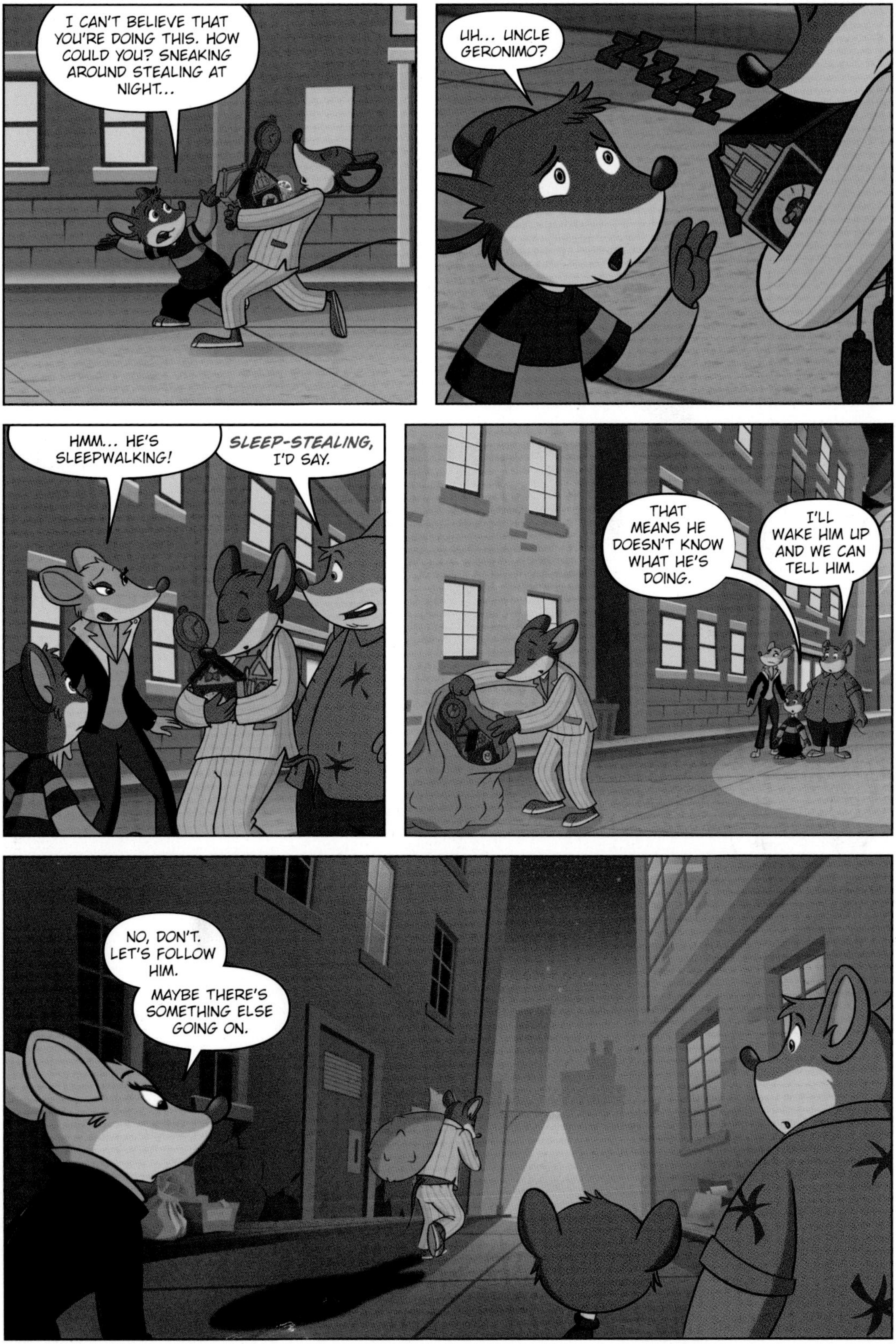
I CAN'T BELIEVE THAT YOU'RE DOING THIS. HOW COULD YOU? SNEAKING AROUND STEALING AT NIGHT...
UH... UNCLE GERONIMO?
ZZZZZ
HMM... HE'S SLEEPWALKING!
SLEEP-STEALING, I'D SAY.
THAT MEANS HE DOESN'T KNOW WHAT HE'S DOING.
I'LL WAKE HIM UP AND WE CAN TELL HIM.
NO, DON'T. LET'S FOLLOW HIM.
MAYBE THERE'S SOMETHING ELSE GOING ON.

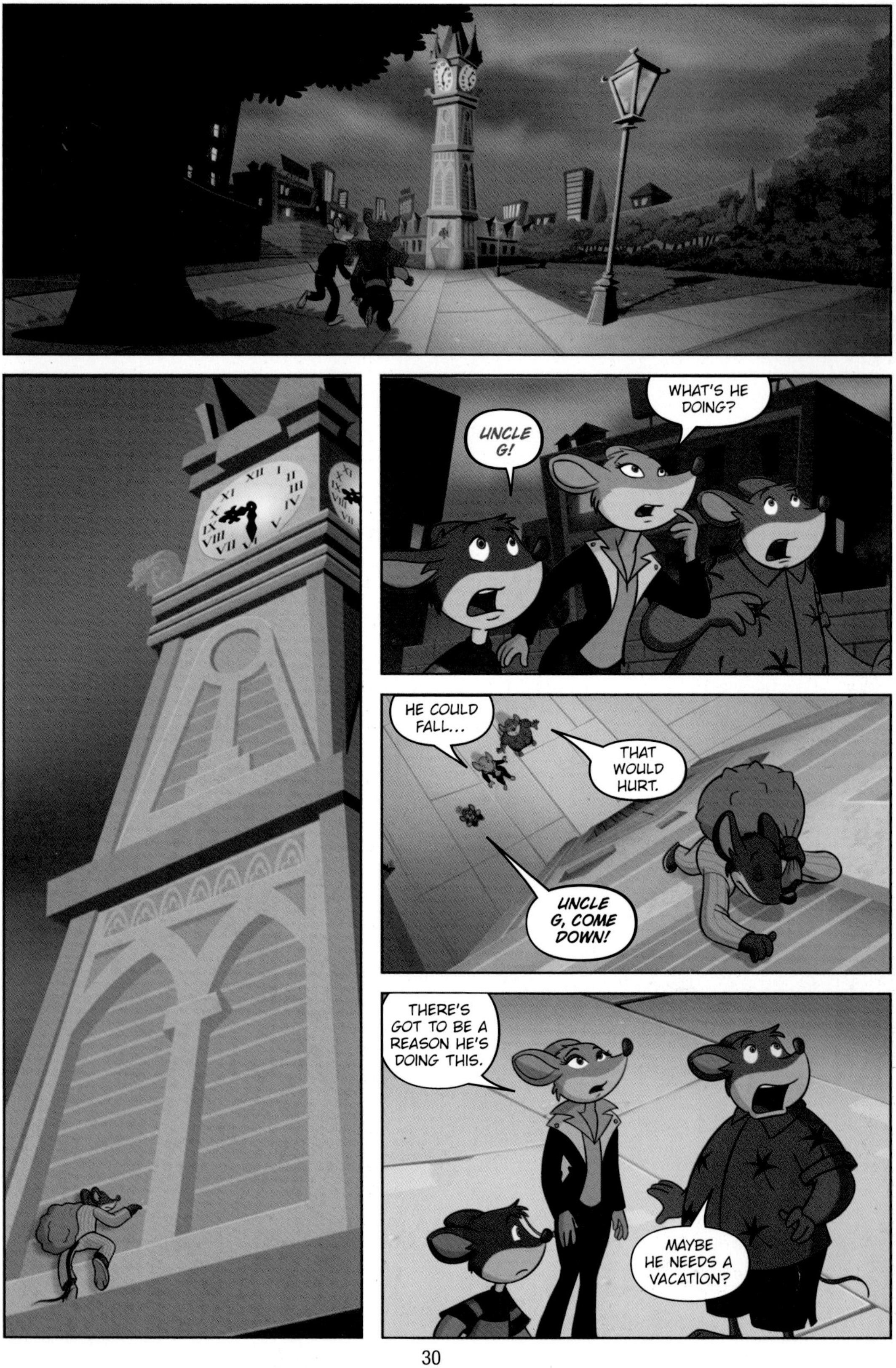
UNCLE G!
WHAT'S HE DOING?
HE COULD FALL...
THAT WOULD HURT.
UNCLE G, COME DOWN!
THERE'S GOT TO BE A REASON HE'S DOING THIS.
MAYBE HE NEEDS A VACATION?

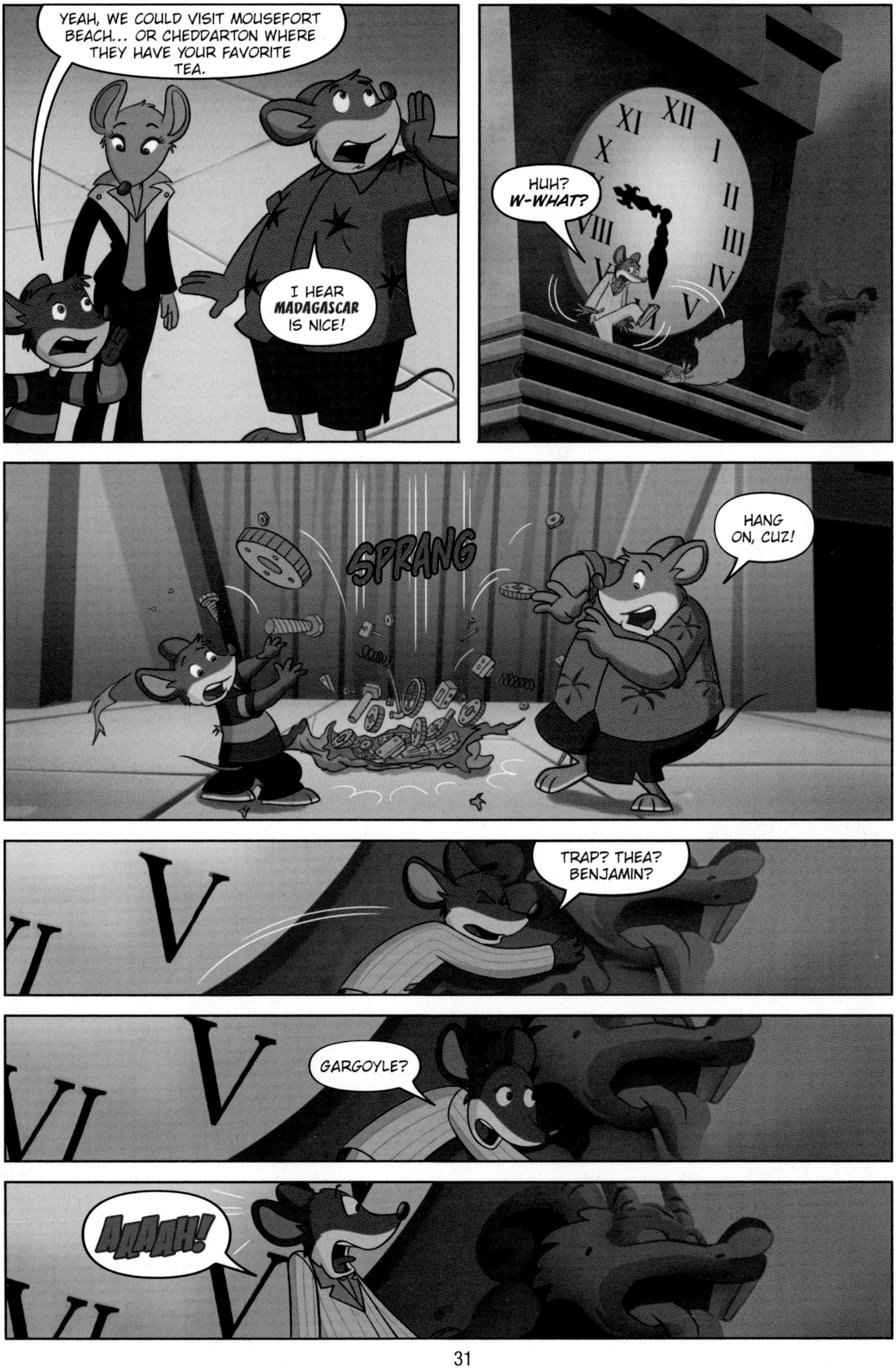
YEAH, WE COULD VISIT MOUSEFORT BEACH... OR CHEDDARTON WHERE THEY HAVE YOUR FAVORITE TEA.
I HEAR MADAGASCAR IS NICE!
HUH? W-WHAT?
SPRANG
HANG ON, CUZ!
TRAP? THEA? BENJAMIN?
GARGOYLE?
AAAAH!

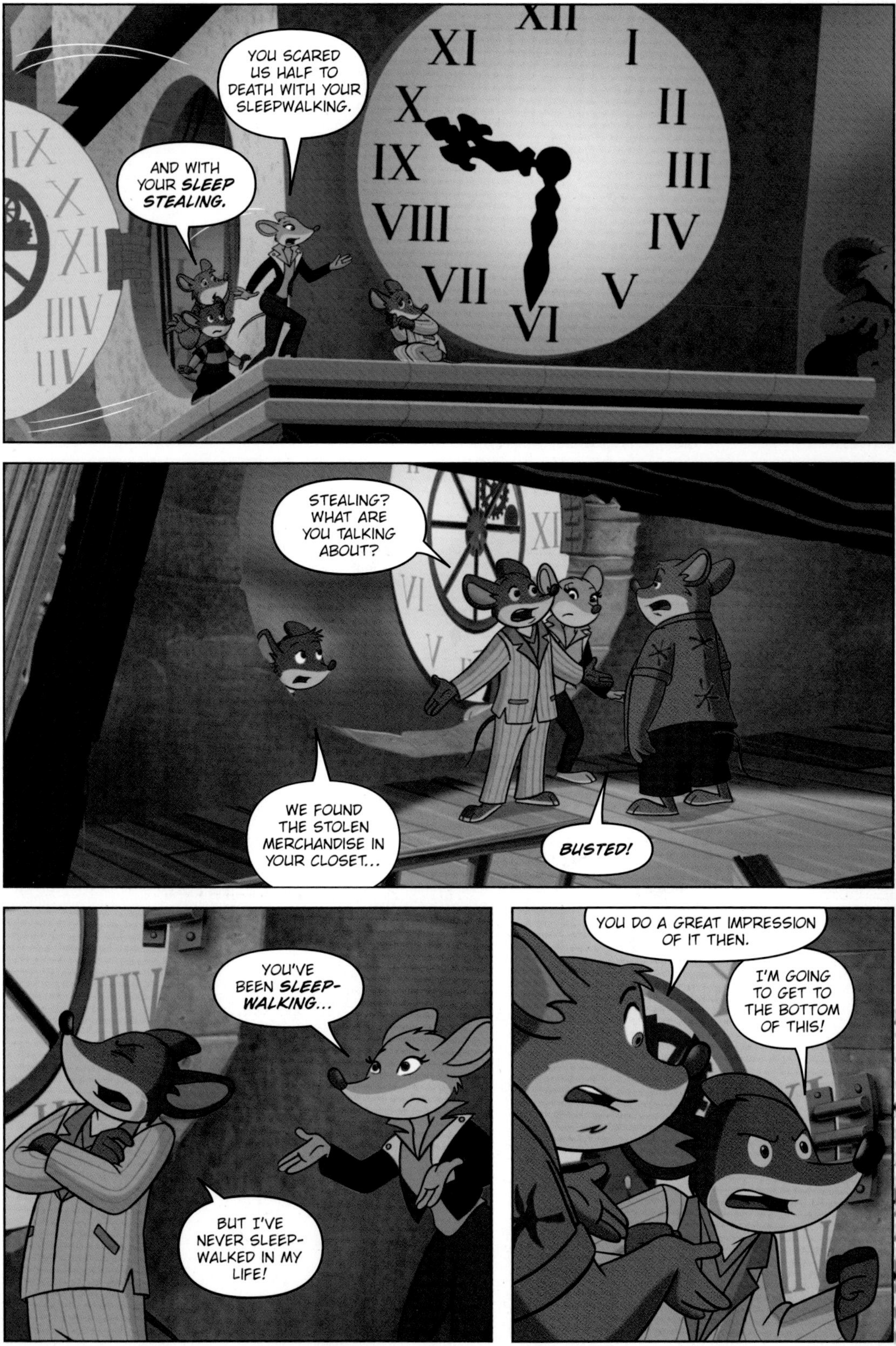
YOU SCARED US HALF TO DEATH WITH YOUR SLEEPWALKING.
AND WITH YOUR **SLEEP STEALING.**
STEALING? WHAT ARE YOU TALKING ABOUT?
WE FOUND THE STOLEN MERCHANDISE IN YOUR CLOSET...
**BUSTED!**
YOU'VE BEEN **SLEEP-WALKING...**
BUT I'VE NEVER SLEEP-WALKED IN MY LIFE!
YOU DO A GREAT IMPRESSION OF IT THEN.
I'M GOING TO GET TO THE BOTTOM OF THIS!

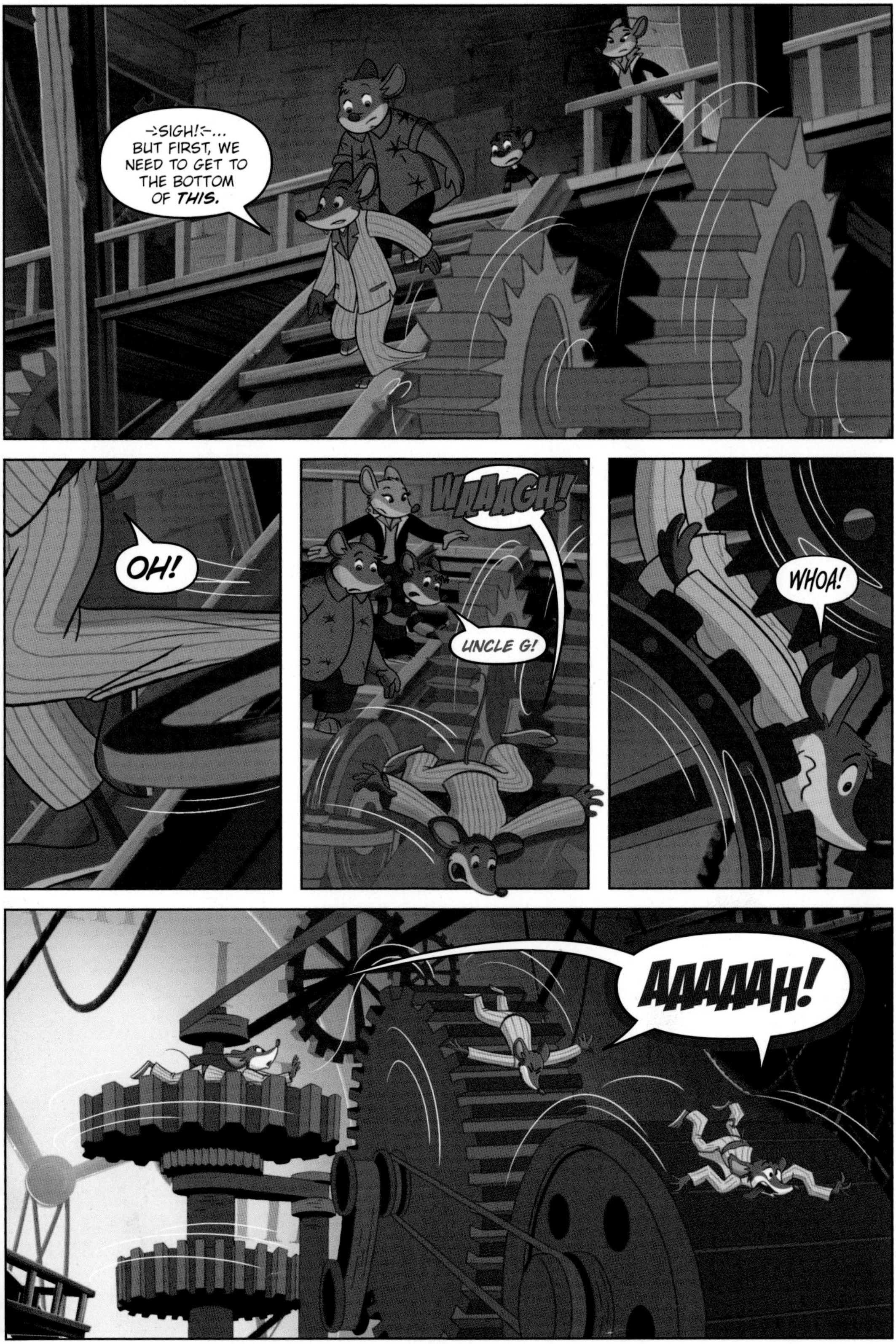

⇒SIGH!⇐... BUT FIRST, WE NEED TO GET TO THE BOTTOM OF THIS.
OH!
WAAAGH!
UNCLE G!
WHOA!
AAAAAH!

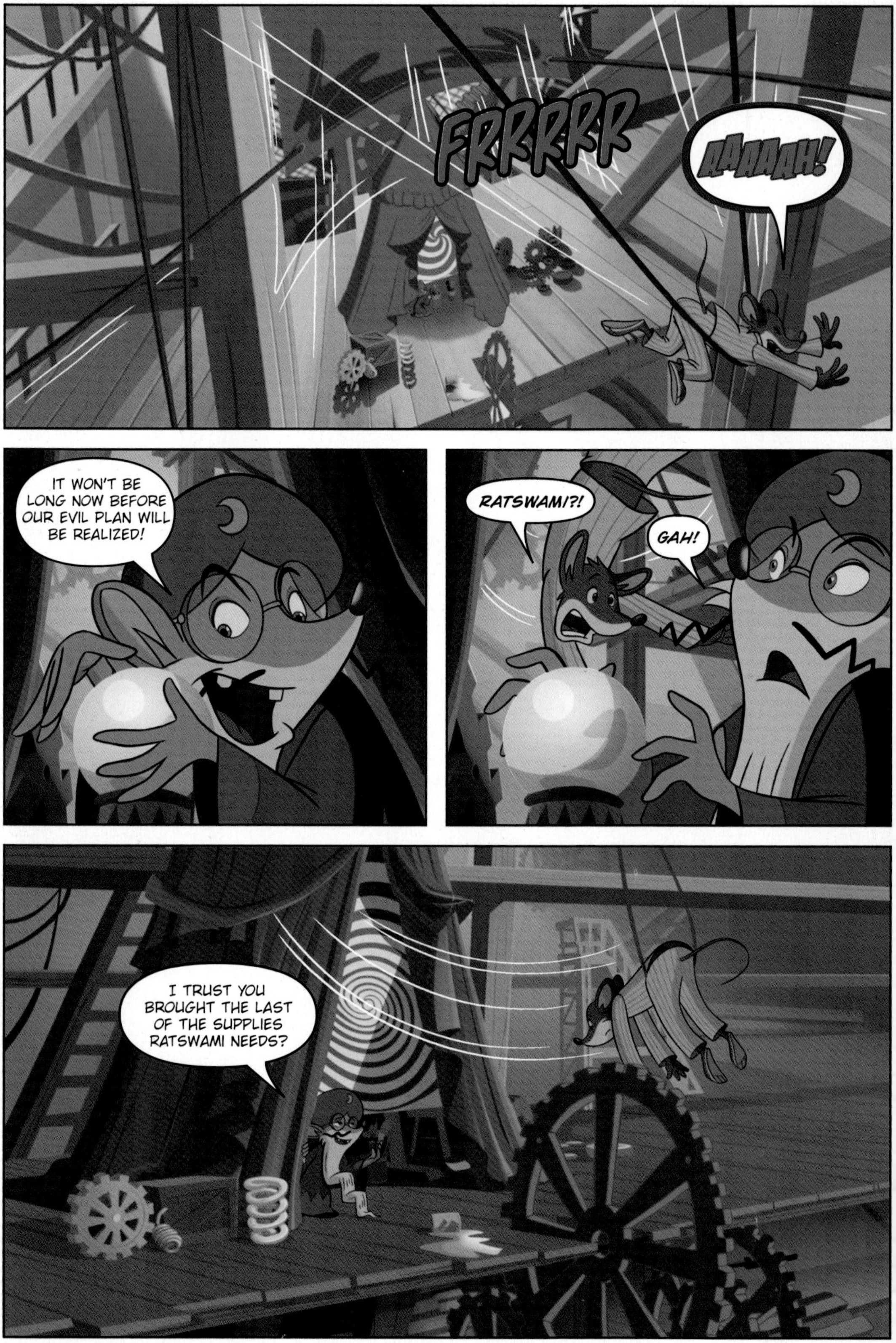

FRRRRR
AAAAAH!
IT WON'T BE LONG NOW BEFORE OUR EVIL PLAN WILL BE REALIZED!
RATSWAMI?!
GAH!
I TRUST YOU BROUGHT THE LAST OF THE SUPPLIES RATSWAMI NEEDS?

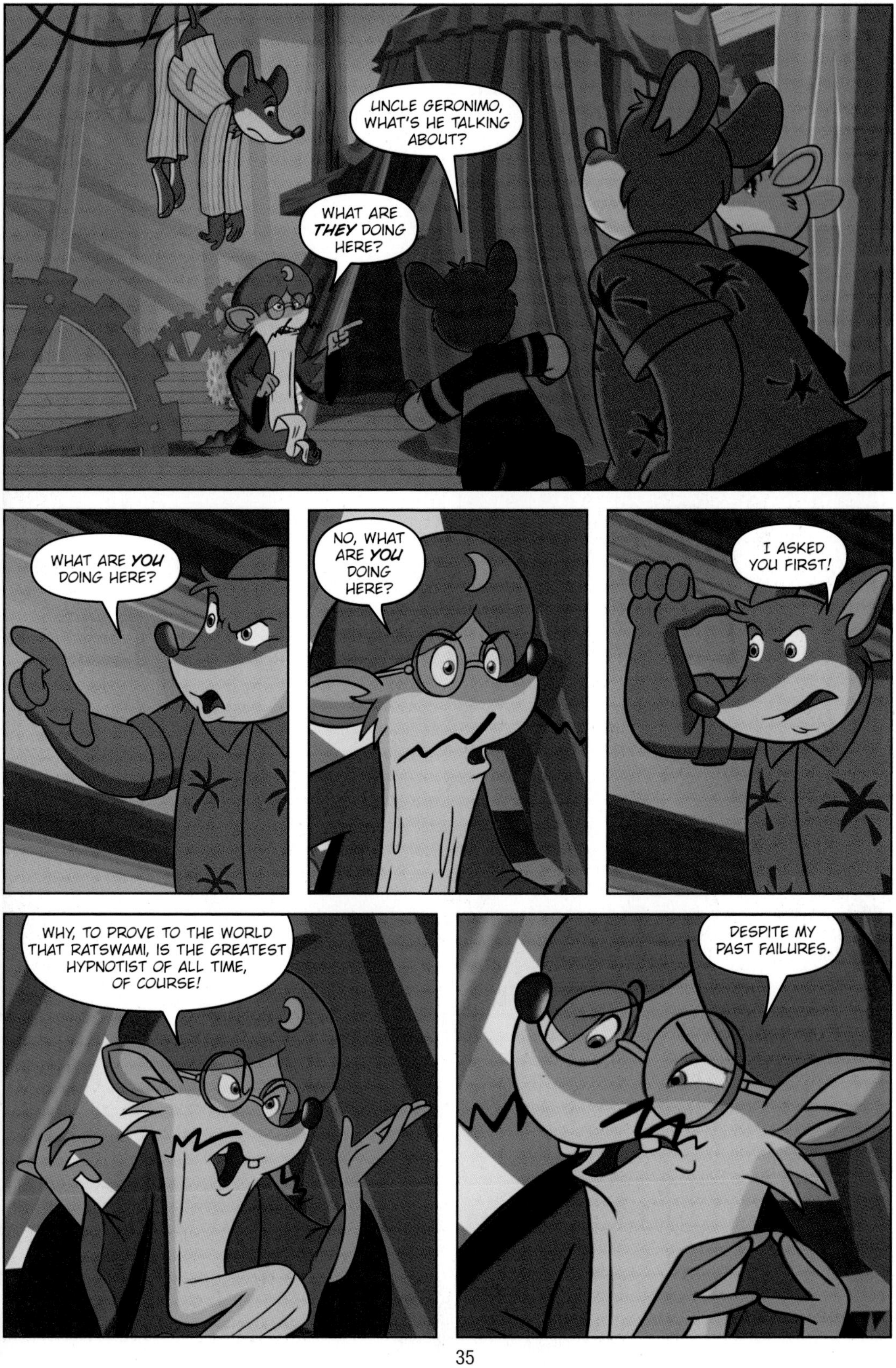
UNCLE GERONIMO, WHAT'S HE TALKING ABOUT?
WHAT ARE *THEY* DOING HERE?
WHAT ARE *YOU* DOING HERE?
NO, WHAT ARE *YOU* DOING HERE?
I ASKED YOU FIRST!
WHY, TO PROVE TO THE WORLD THAT RATSWAMI, IS THE GREATEST HYPNOTIST OF ALL TIME, OF COURSE!
DESPITE MY PAST FAILURES.

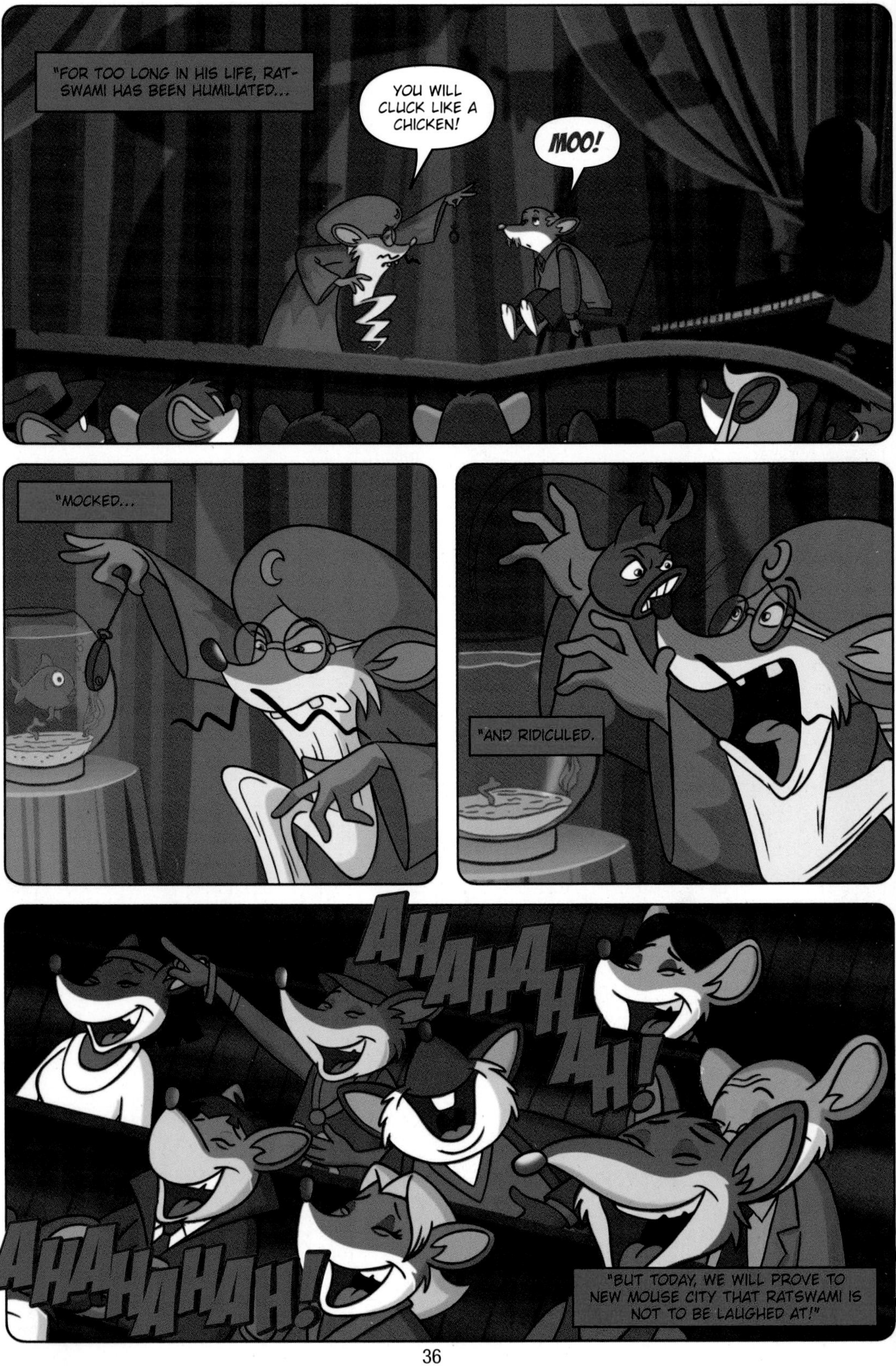
"FOR TOO LONG IN HIS LIFE, RAT-SWAMI HAS BEEN HUMILIATED...
YOU WILL CLUCK LIKE A CHICKEN!
MOO!
"MOCKED...
"AND RIDICULED.
AHAHAHAHAH!
AHAHAHAHAH!
"BUT TODAY, WE WILL PROVE TO NEW MOUSE CITY THAT RATSWAMI IS NOT TO BE LAUGHED AT!"

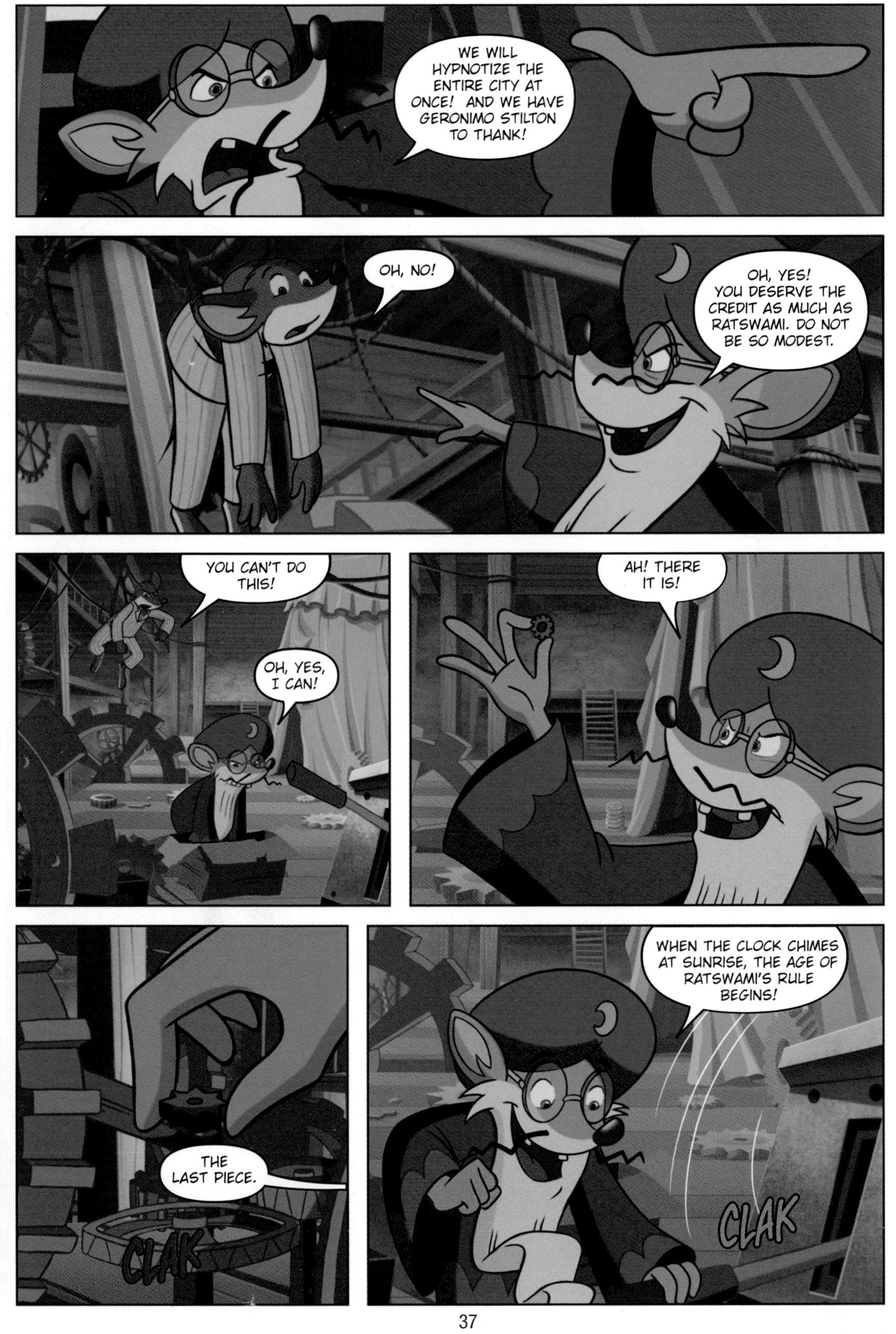
WE WILL HYPNOTIZE THE ENTIRE CITY AT ONCE! AND WE HAVE GERONIMO STILTON TO THANK!
OH, NO!
OH, YES! YOU DESERVE THE CREDIT AS MUCH AS RATSWAMI. DO NOT BE SO MODEST.
YOU CAN'T DO THIS!
OH, YES, I CAN!
AH! THERE IT IS!
THE LAST PIECE.
CLAK
WHEN THE CLOCK CHIMES AT SUNRISE, THE AGE OF RATSWAMI'S RULE BEGINS!
CLAK

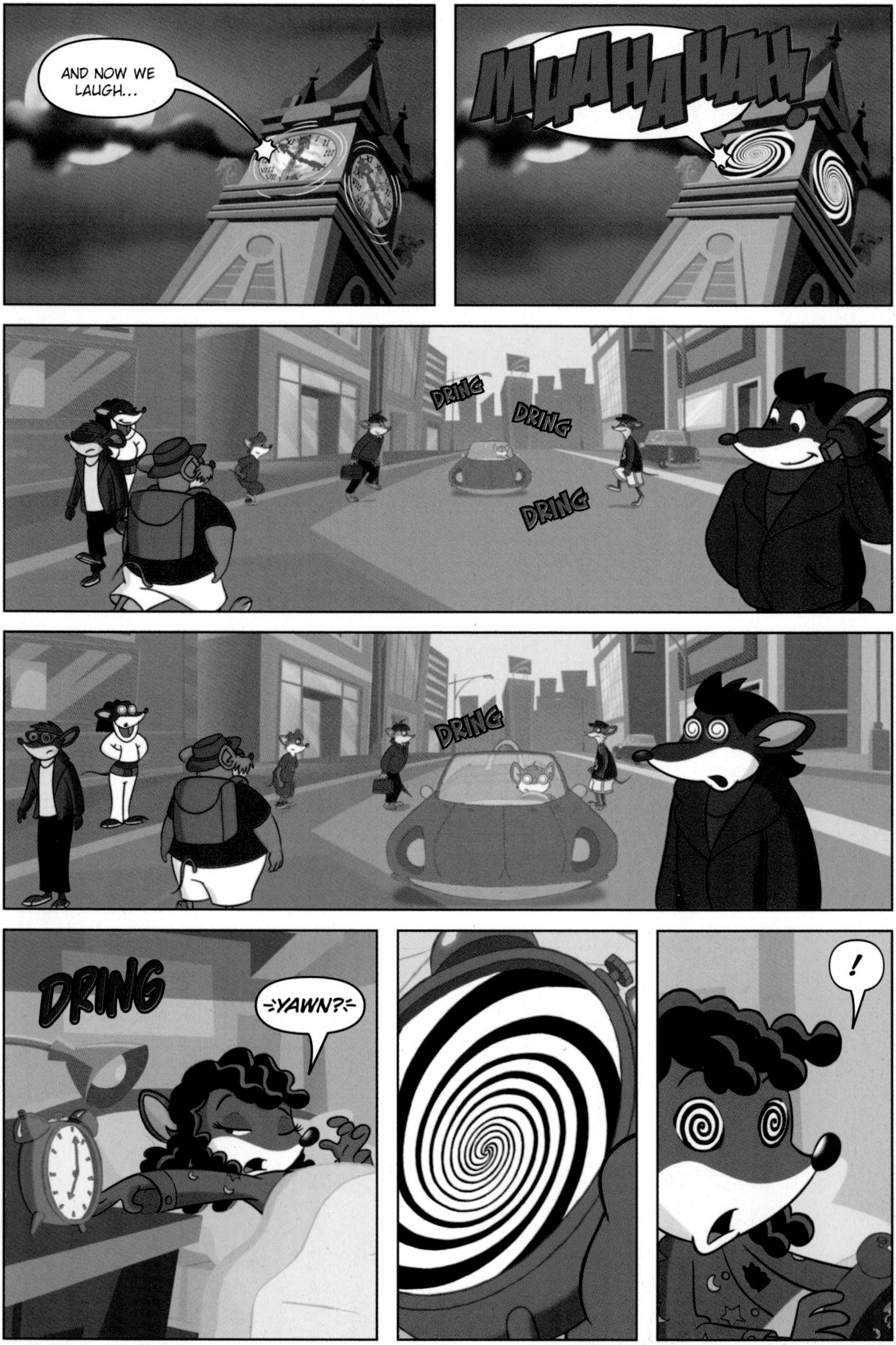

AND NOW WE LAUGH...
MUAHAHAH!
DRING
DRING
DRING
DRING
DRING
YAWN?
!

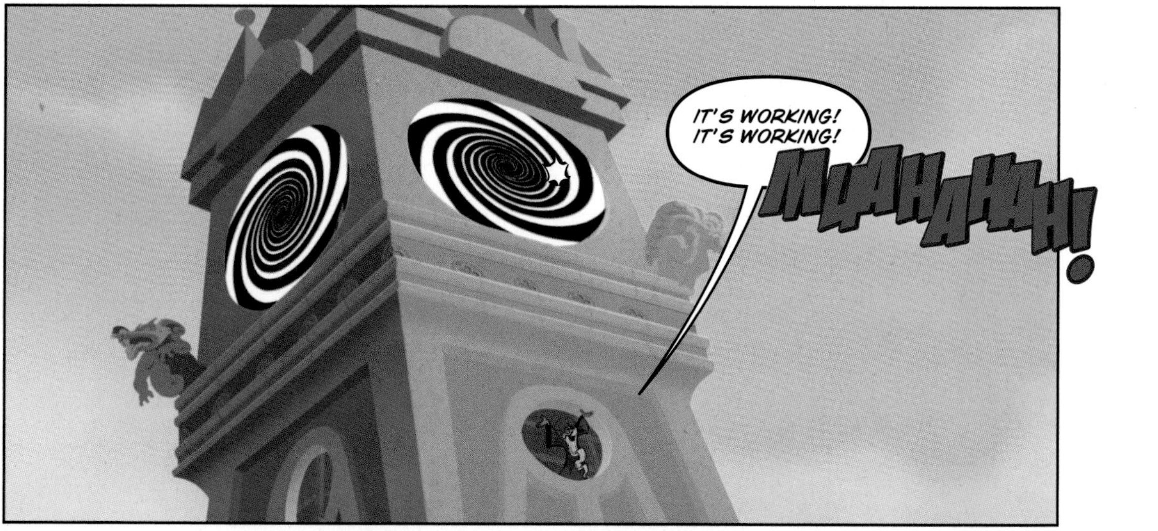
IT'S WORKING! IT'S WORKING!
MUAHAHAH!

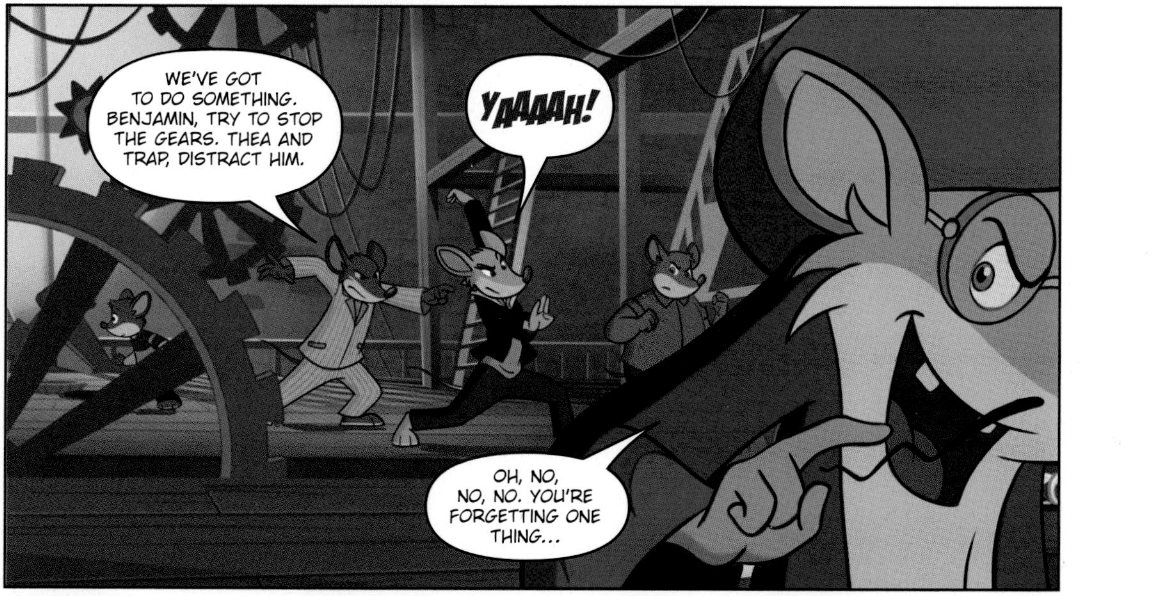
WE'VE GOT TO DO SOMETHING. BENJAMIN, TRY TO STOP THE GEARS. THEA AND TRAP, DISTRACT HIM.
YAAAAH!
OH, NO, NO, NO. YOU'RE FORGETTING ONE THING...

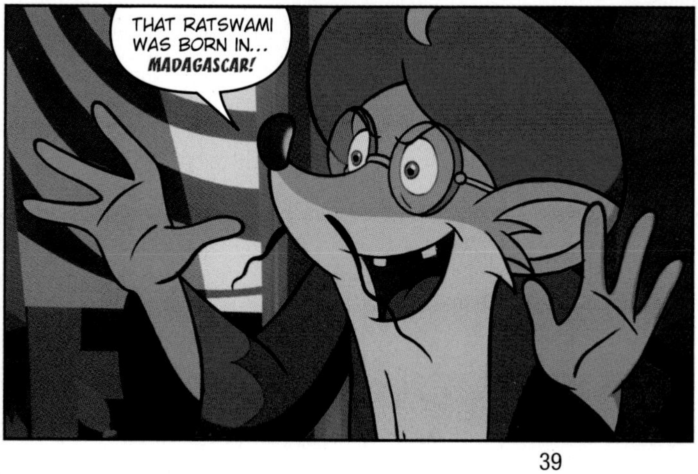
THAT RATSWAMI WAS BORN IN... MADAGASCAR!

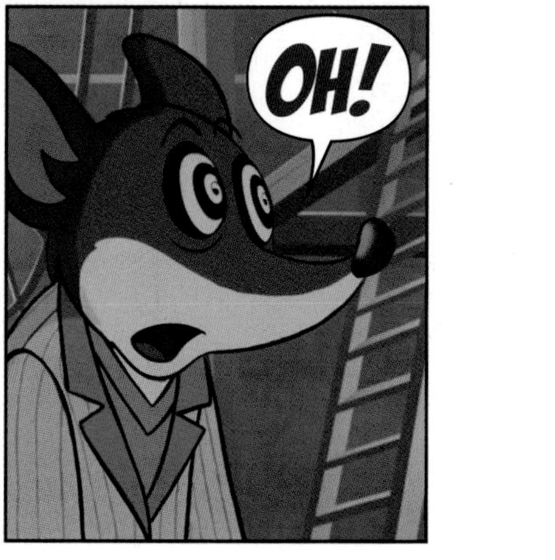
OH!

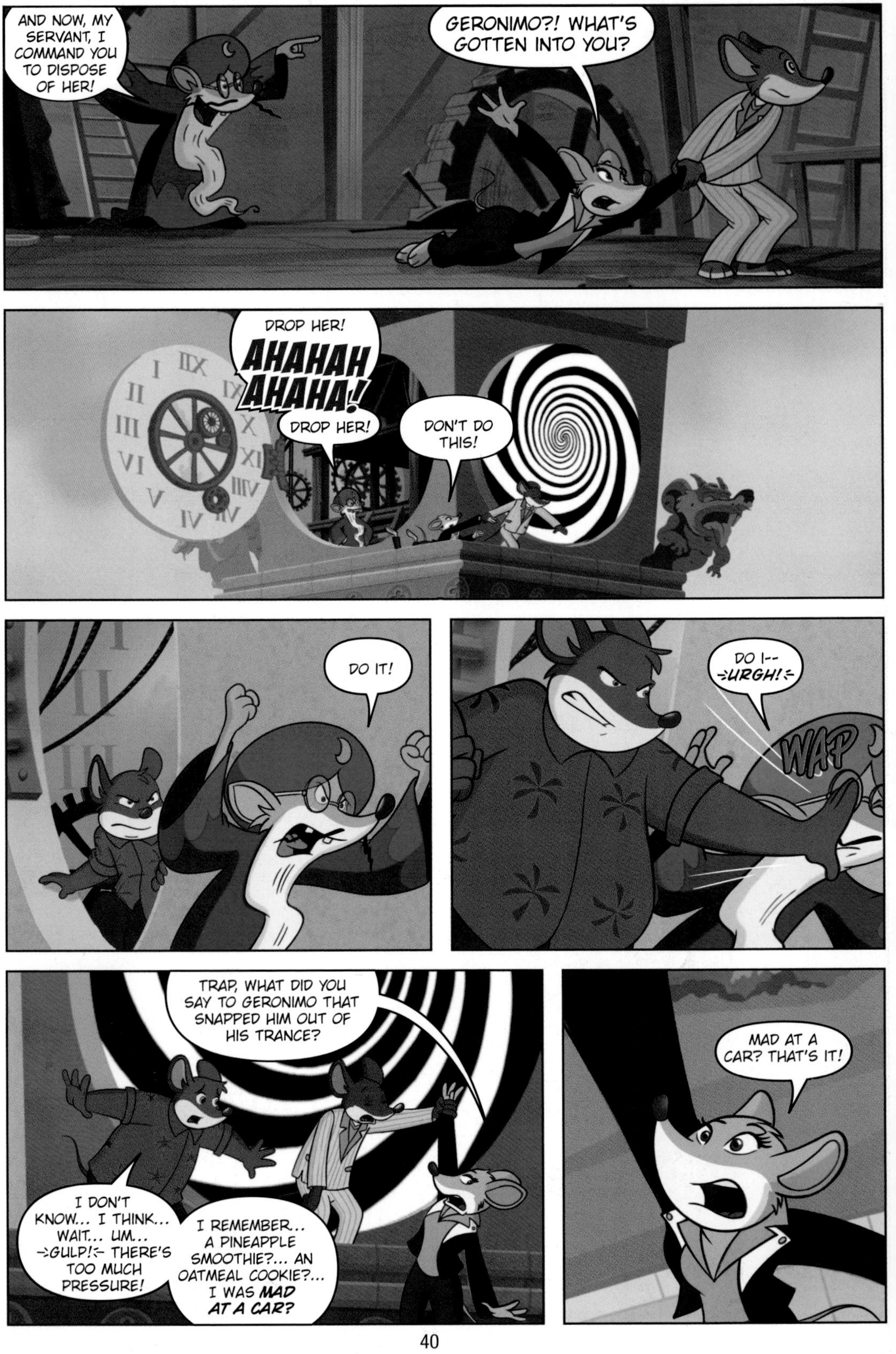
AND NOW, MY SERVANT, I COMMAND YOU TO DISPOSE OF HER!
GERONIMO?! WHAT'S GOTTEN INTO YOU?
DROP HER!
AHAHAH AHAHA!
DROP HER!
DON'T DO THIS!
DO IT!
DO I-- -URGH!-
WAP
TRAP, WHAT DID YOU SAY TO GERONIMO THAT SNAPPED HIM OUT OF HIS TRANCE?
I DON'T KNOW... I THINK... WAIT... UM... -GULP!- THERE'S TOO MUCH PRESSURE!
I REMEMBER... A PINEAPPLE SMOOTHIE?... AN OATMEAL COOKIE?... I WAS MAD AT A CAR?
MAD AT A CAR? THAT'S IT!

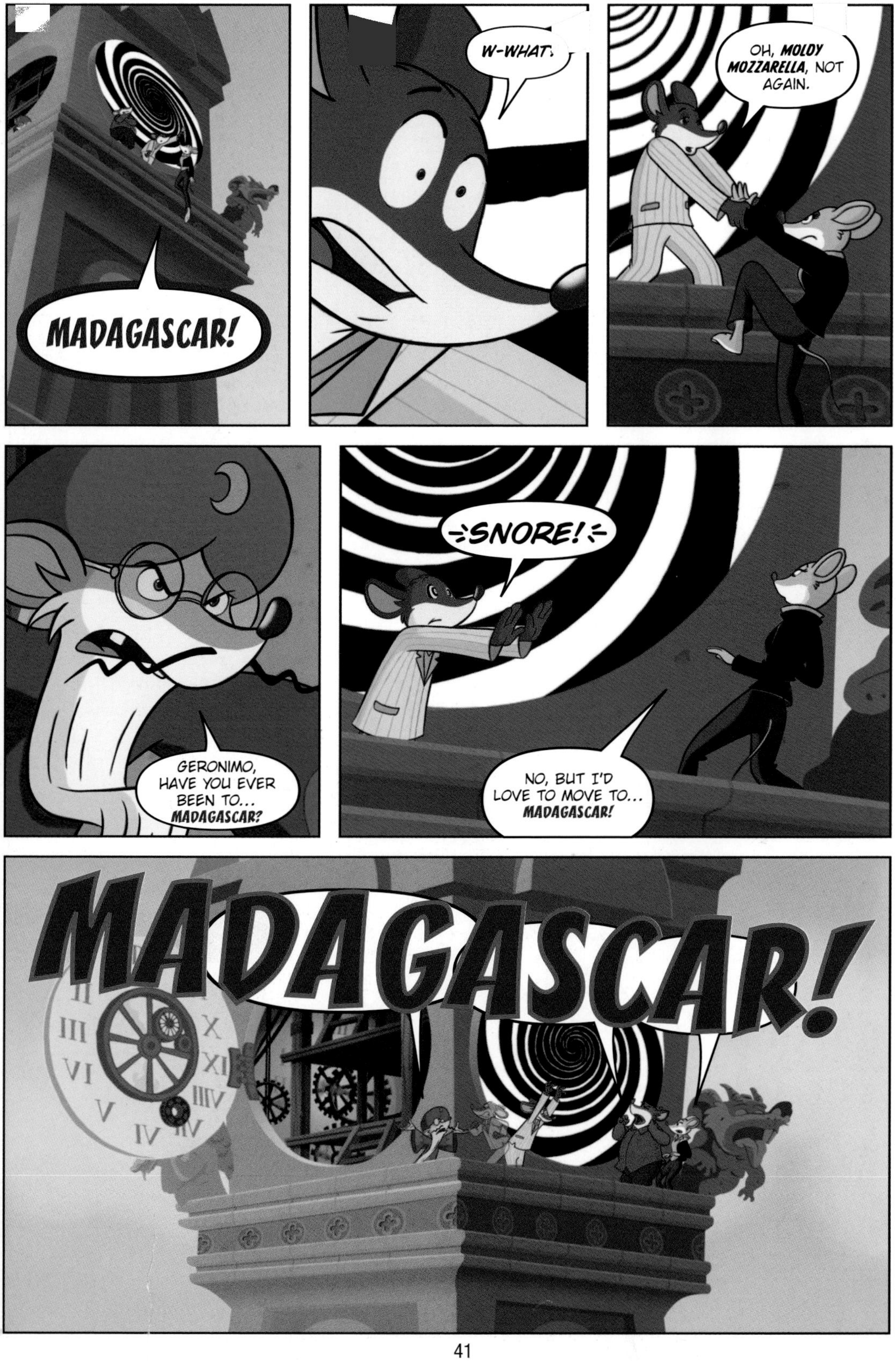

MADAGASCAR!
W-WHAT
OH, MOLDY MOZZARELLA, NOT AGAIN.
GERONIMO, HAVE YOU EVER BEEN TO... MADAGASCAR?
SNORE!
NO, BUT I'D LOVE TO MOVE TO... MADAGASCAR!
MADAGASCAR!

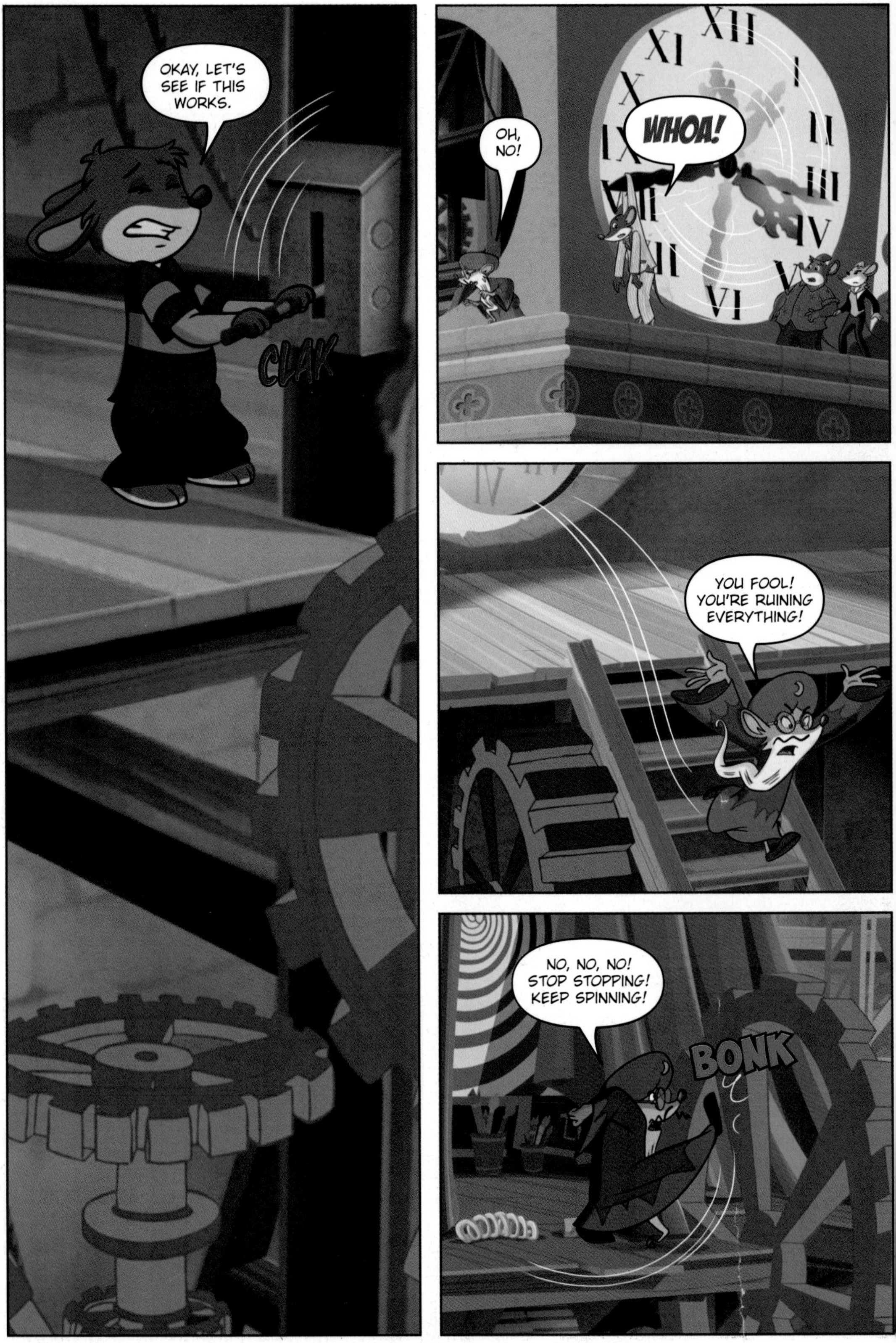
OKAY, LET'S SEE IF THIS WORKS.
CLAK
OH, NO!
WHOA!
YOU FOOL! YOU'RE RUINING EVERYTHING!
NO, NO, NO! STOP STOPPING! KEEP SPINNING!
BONK

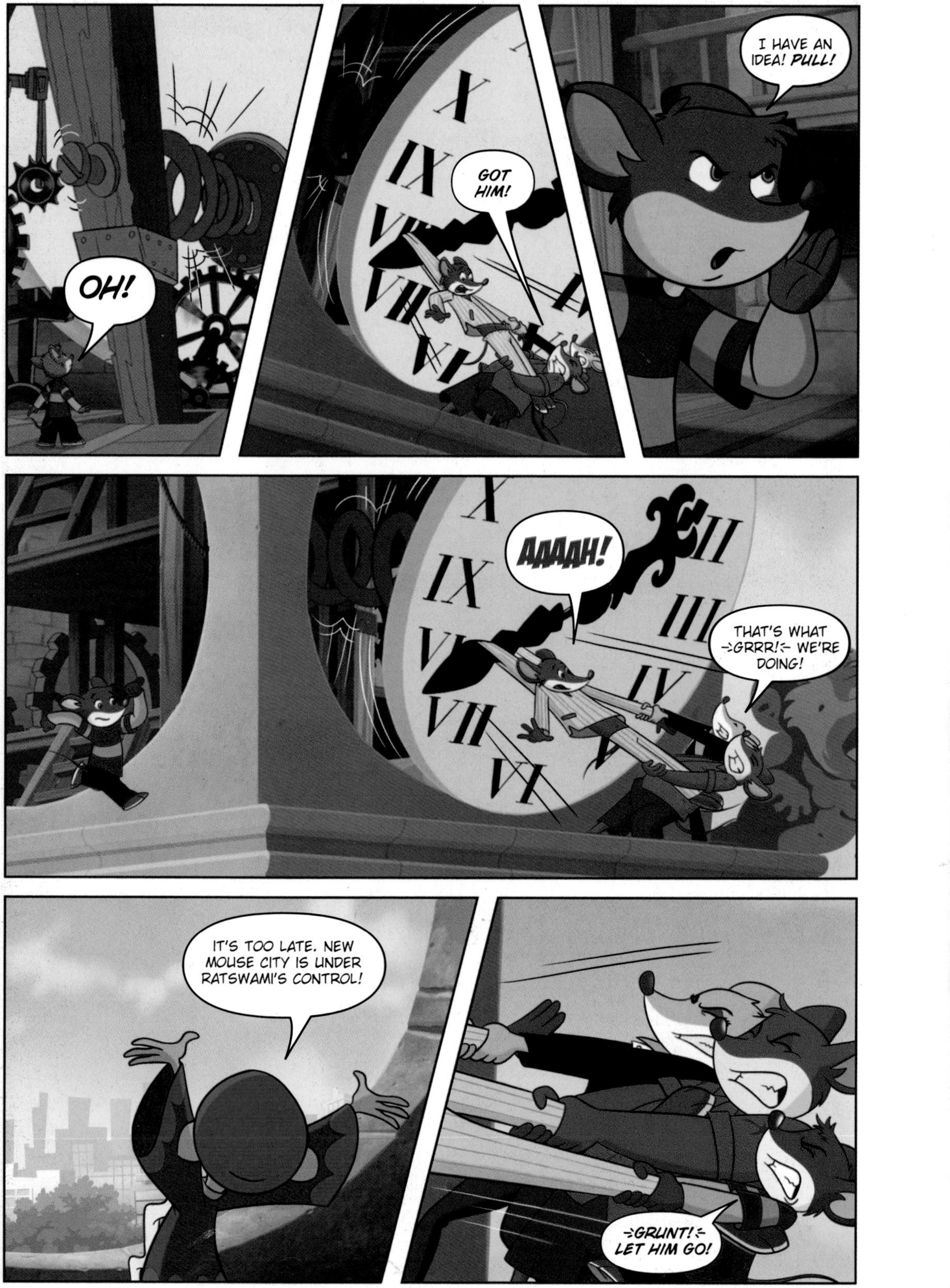
OH!
GOT HIM!
I HAVE AN IDEA! PULL!
AAAAH!
THAT'S WHAT =GRRR!= WE'RE DOING!
IT'S TOO LATE. NEW MOUSE CITY IS UNDER RATSWAMI'S CONTROL!
=GRUNT!= LET HIM GO!

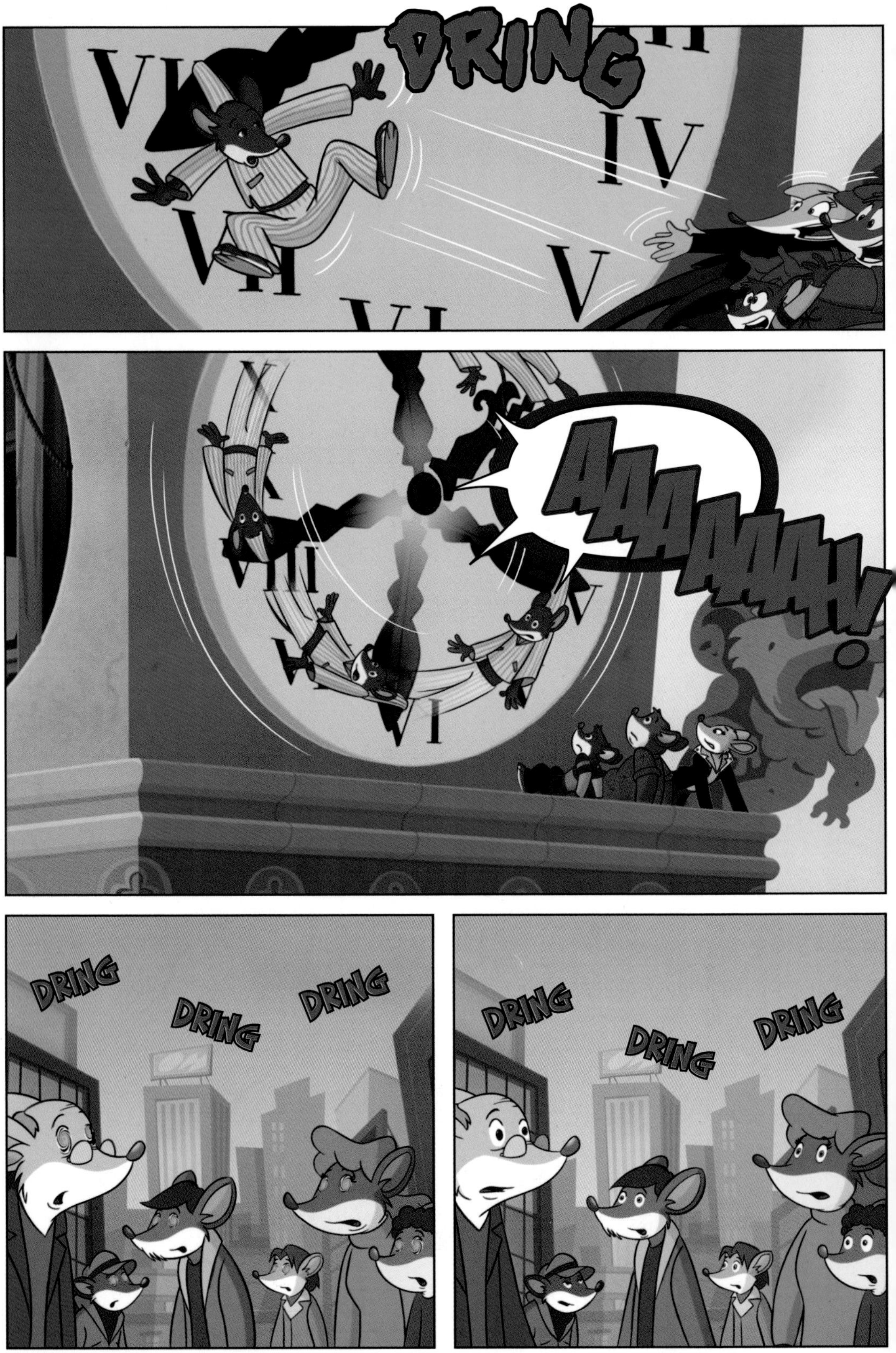
DRING
AAAAAAAH!
DRING
DRING
DRING
DRING
DRING
DRING

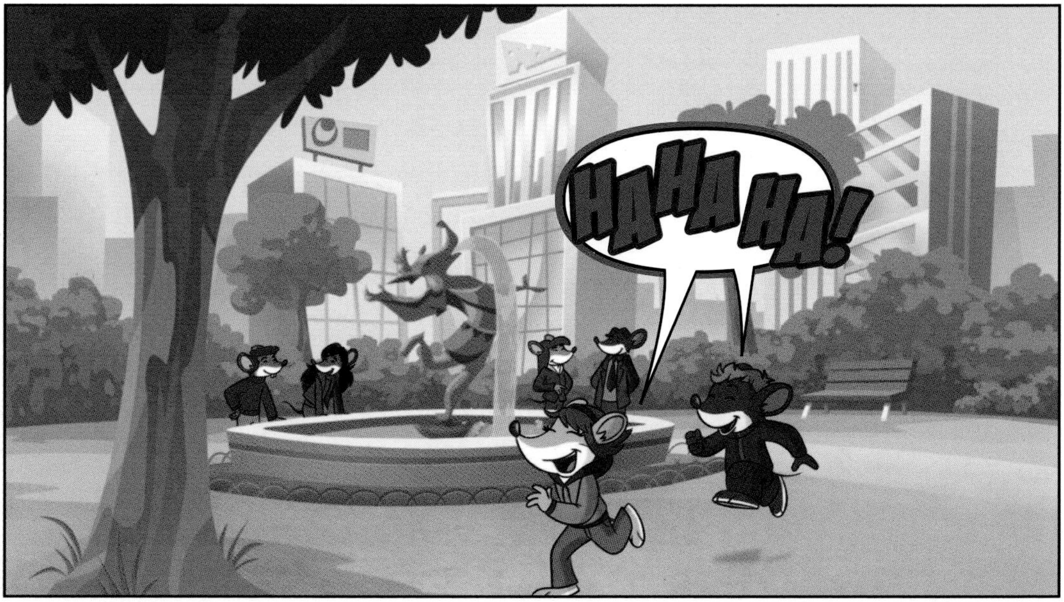
HAHAHA!

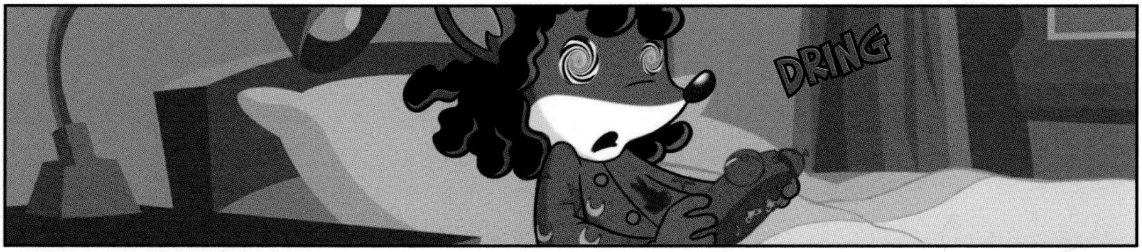
DRING

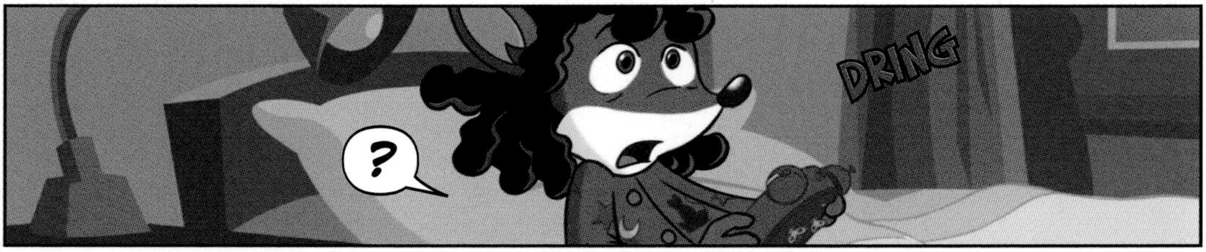
?
DRING

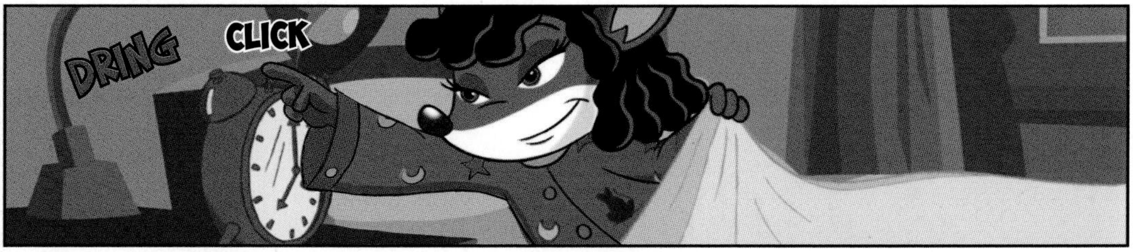
DRING
CLICK

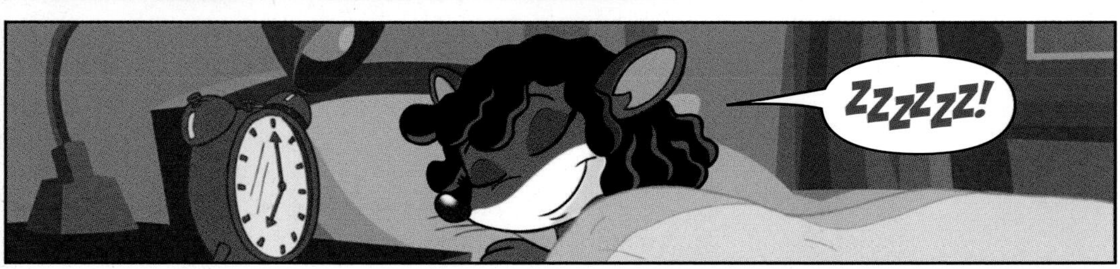
ZZZZZZ!

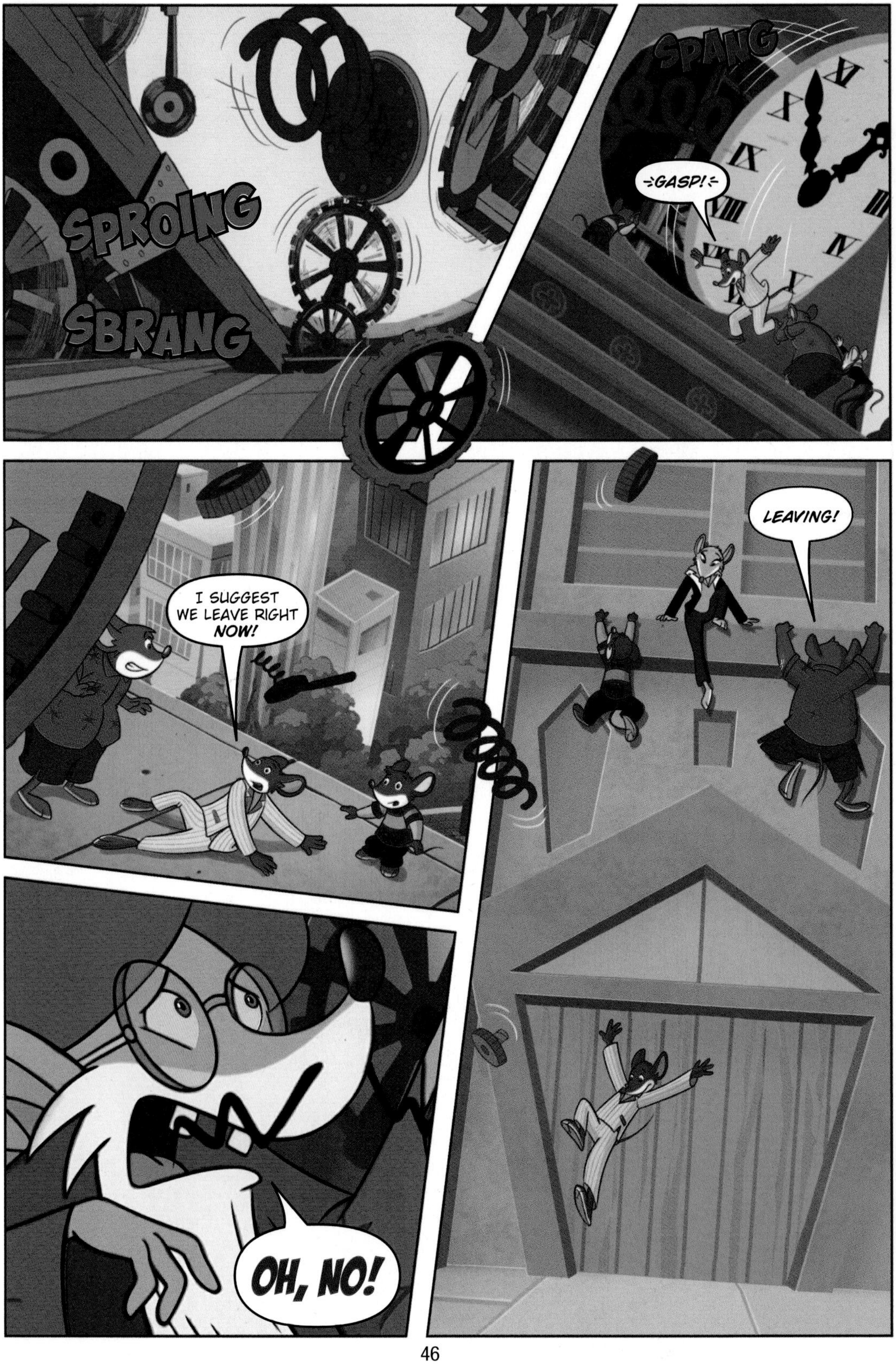
SPROING
SBRANG
SPANG
GASP!
I SUGGEST WE LEAVE RIGHT NOW!
LEAVING!
OH, NO!

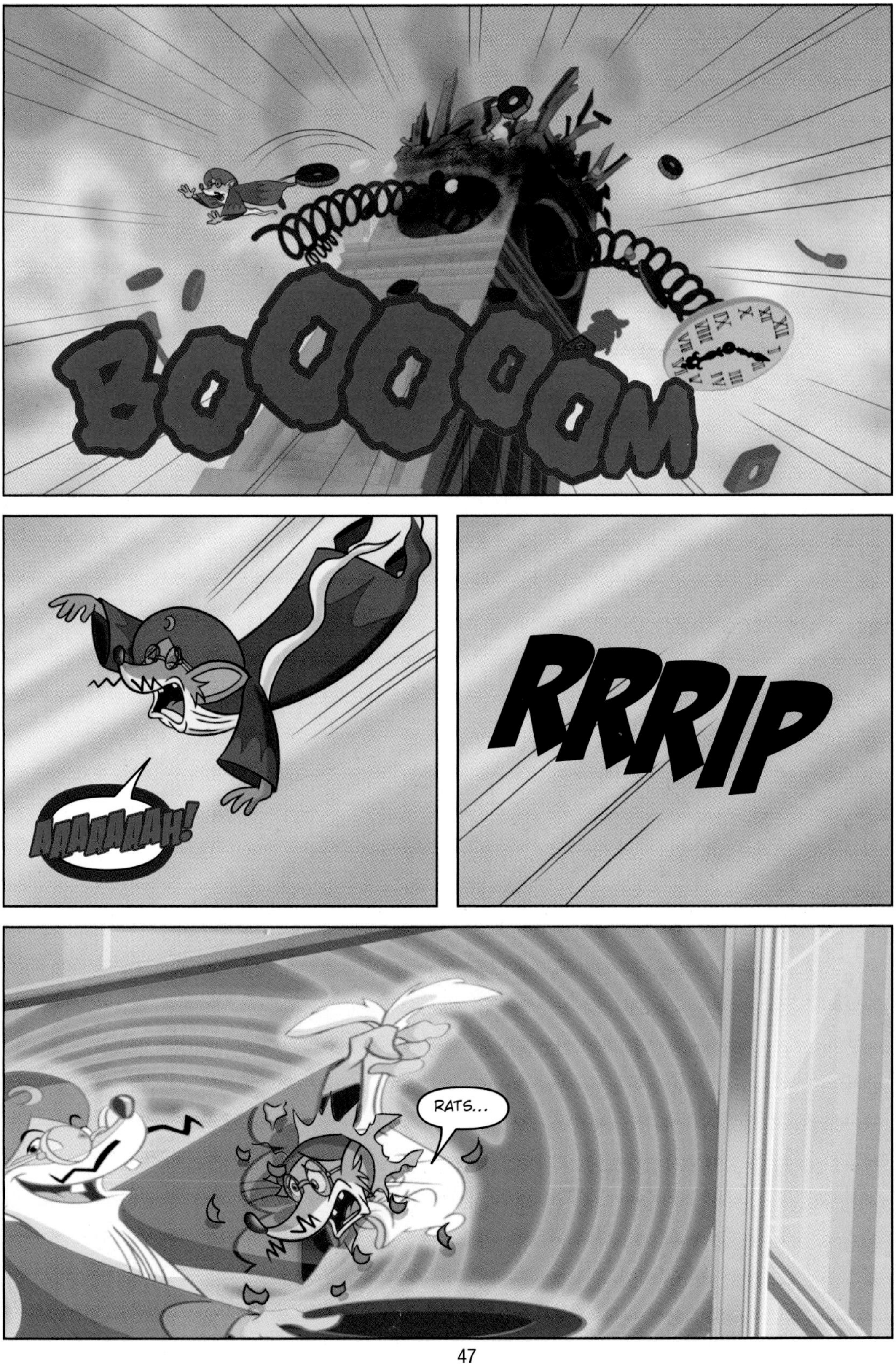
BOOOOOOM
AAAAAAAH!
RRRIP
RATS...

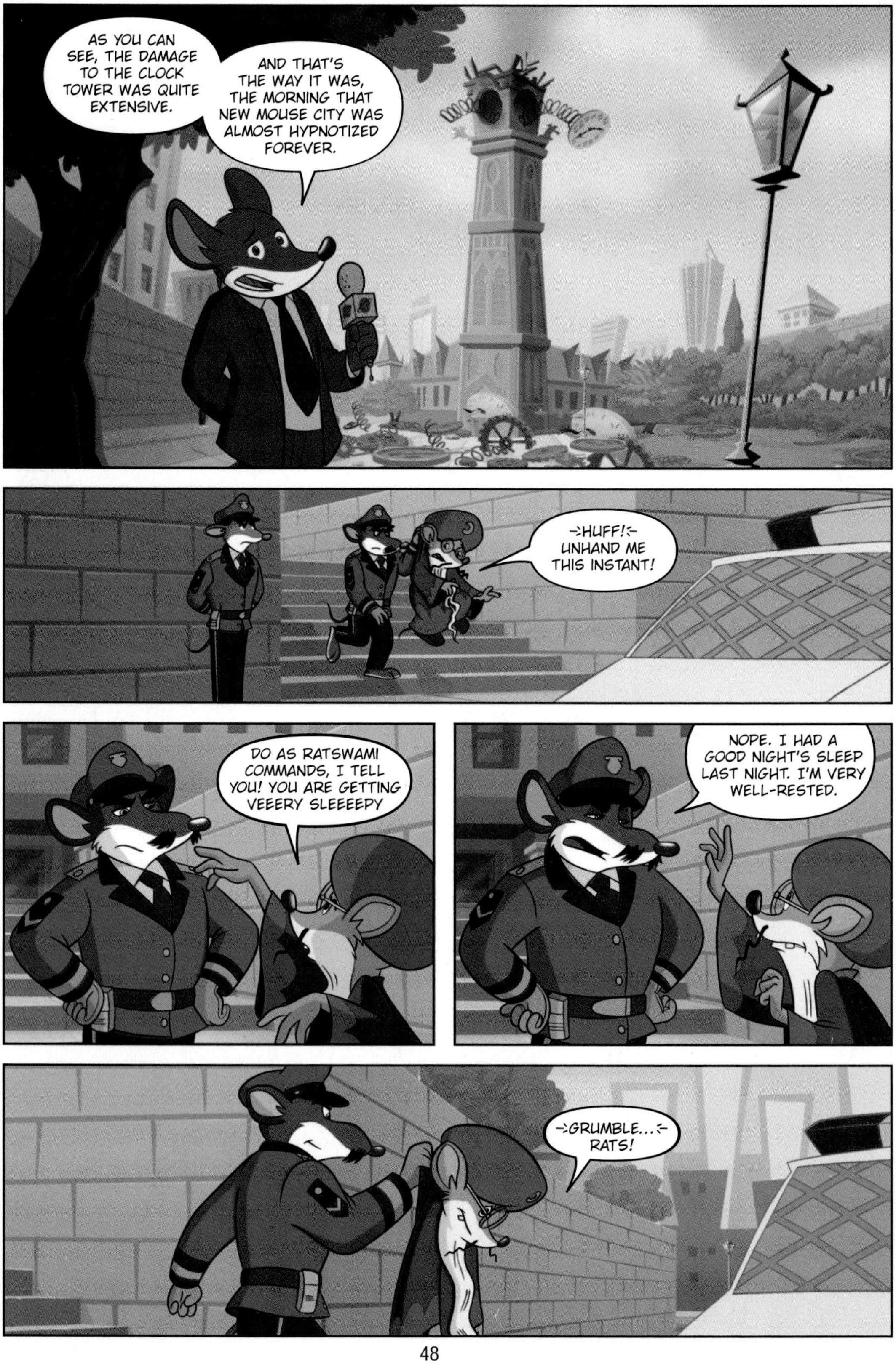
AS YOU CAN SEE, THE DAMAGE TO THE CLOCK TOWER WAS QUITE EXTENSIVE.
AND THAT'S THE WAY IT WAS, THE MORNING THAT NEW MOUSE CITY WAS ALMOST HYPNOTIZED FOREVER.
HUFF! UNHAND ME THIS INSTANT!
DO AS RATSWAMI COMMANDS, I TELL YOU! YOU ARE GETTING VEEERY SLEEEEPY
NOPE. I HAD A GOOD NIGHT'S SLEEP LAST NIGHT. I'M VERY WELL-RESTED.
GRUMBLE... RATS!

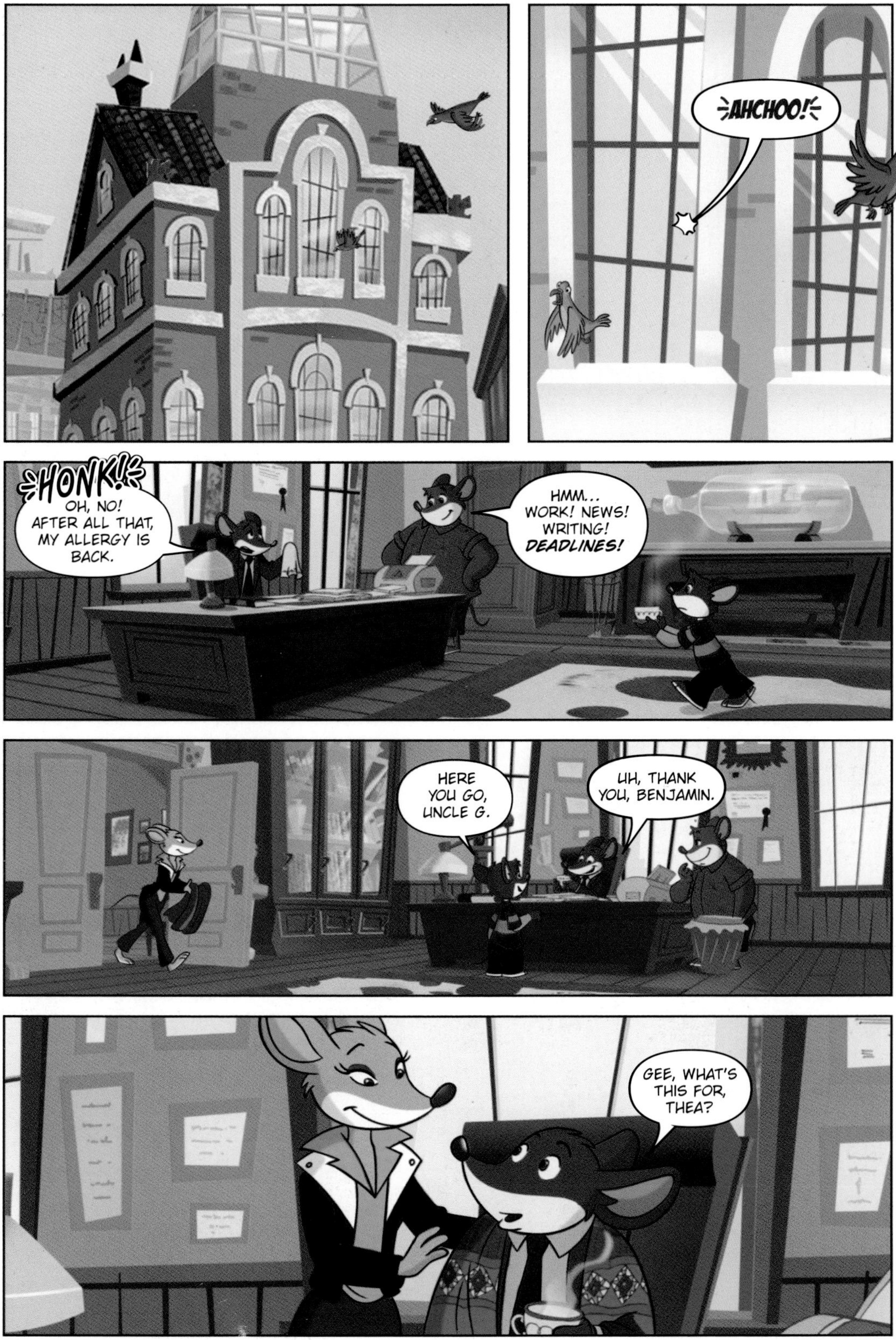

AHCHOO!
HONK!
OH, NO! AFTER ALL THAT, MY ALLERGY IS BACK.
HMM... WORK! NEWS! WRITING! DEADLINES!
HERE YOU GO, UNCLE G.
UH, THANK YOU, BENJAMIN.
GEE, WHAT'S THIS FOR, THEA?

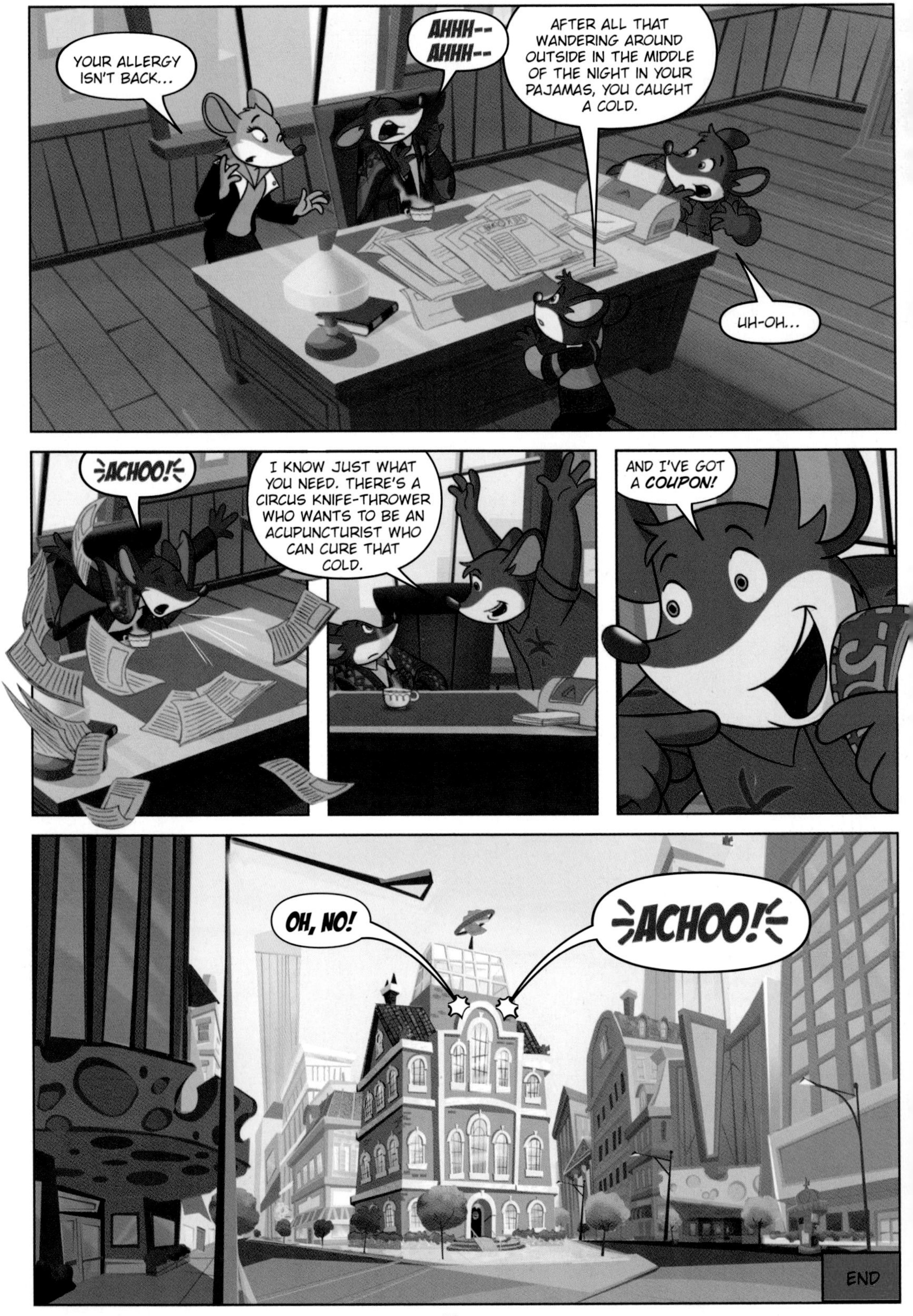
YOUR ALLERGY ISN'T BACK...
AHHH-- AHHH--
AFTER ALL THAT WANDERING AROUND OUTSIDE IN THE MIDDLE OF THE NIGHT IN YOUR PAJAMAS, YOU CAUGHT A COLD.
UH-OH...
ACHOO!
I KNOW JUST WHAT YOU NEED. THERE'S A CIRCUS KNIFE-THROWER WHO WANTS TO BE AN ACUPUNCTURIST WHO CAN CURE THAT COLD.
AND I'VE GOT A COUPON!
OH, NO!
ACHOO!
END

# Watch Out For PAPERCUTZ™

Welcome to the eerily engaging eighth GERONIMO STILTON REPORTER graphic novel, "Hypno-Tick Tock" (not to be confused with any addictive form of social media!), the official comics adaptation of the eighth episode of *Geronimo Stilton*, Season One, written by Charlotte Fullerton, brought to you by Papercutz—those cheesy characters dedicated to publishing great graphic novels for all ages. I'm Salicrup, *Jim Salicrup*, the Editor-in-Chief and Trap Stilton's Fashion Consultant, here once again with more of *The Philosophy of Geronimo Stilton*. Essentially this philosophy is the guiding principles behind the creation of every Geronimo Stilton story, whether created for books, animation, or comics. You can check out the entire *Philosophy of Geronimo Stilton* online at geronimostilton.com. So, now, without further ado, let's examine the next section of the *Philosophy*…

GERONIMO STILTON AND MAGIC
Magic is just a negative illusion! A magic wand is not enough to change reality or to transform things that we don't want to accept. Since the dawn of time man has tried to find help in magic to resolve problems… but magic doesn't exist! Magic amulets are useless, magic spells don't work… and witches, wizards, fairies, elves, gnomes, ogres, and giants only exist in fairy tales and we can only accept them as protagonists of imaginative stories.

Gee, that's a little disillusioning, isn't it? Didn't we just say in GERONIMO STILTON REPORTER #7 that "using your imagination can feel like magic—for example, if you made up a story and wrote it down, you've created something that didn't exist before. It's really a wonderful feeling when you visualize an idea in your mind and then turn it into something real."
But I guess it all depends on your definition of magic. While stage magicians are indeed creating illusions, are they necessarily "negative"? If the true goal is to astound and amaze an audience, to make them wonder exactly how the magician pulled off his trick, what's wrong with that? Of course, if someone, say, a dishonest fortune

teller, took advantage of a person by pretending to offer up false hope in exchange for money, that's certainly not magic. That's a combination of greed and cruelty. That's not a fortune teller, that's a con artist. And I guess what this part of the philosophy is really saying is that turning to the supernatural to deal with real-life problems of any kind is a big mistake. That the lesson to be learned from Geronimo Stilton, is that we all have to find real solutions to real problems.
But, you may ask, did Geronimo Stilton resort to hypnotism to deal with his "work allergy"? Yes, he did, but hypnotism is actually real, although the extent of it is often greatly exaggerated in fiction. In real life, people will go to hypnotists to help them with problems such as quitting smoking or to provide the will power to stick to a weight loss diet. Hypnotizing an entire city is not possible, it's just a fanciful idea that helps make for "imaginative stories."
Speaking of imaginative stories, we suggest that you don't miss GERONIMO STILTON REPORTER #9 "The Mask of Rat-Jitsu." Check out the special preview starting on the next page. Hey, this is almost like being a fortune-teller…turn the page and get a glimpse into Geronimo's future! It could be a part of your future too, if you decide to join us—it'll be available from booksellers and libraries everywhere… as if by magic!

Thanks,

*Jim*

## STAY IN TOUCH!

EMAIL:        salicrup@papercutz.com
WEB:          papercutz.com
TWITTER:      @papercutzgn
INSTAGRAM:    @papercutzgn
FACEBOOK:     PAPERCUTZGRAPHICNOVELS
SNAIL MAIL:   Papercutz, 160 Broadway, Suite 700, East Wing, New York, NY 10038

Go to papercutz.com and sign up for the free Papercutz e-newsletter!

**Special Preview of GERONIMO STILTON REPORTER Graphic Novel #9**
**"The Mask of Rat-Jitsu"!**

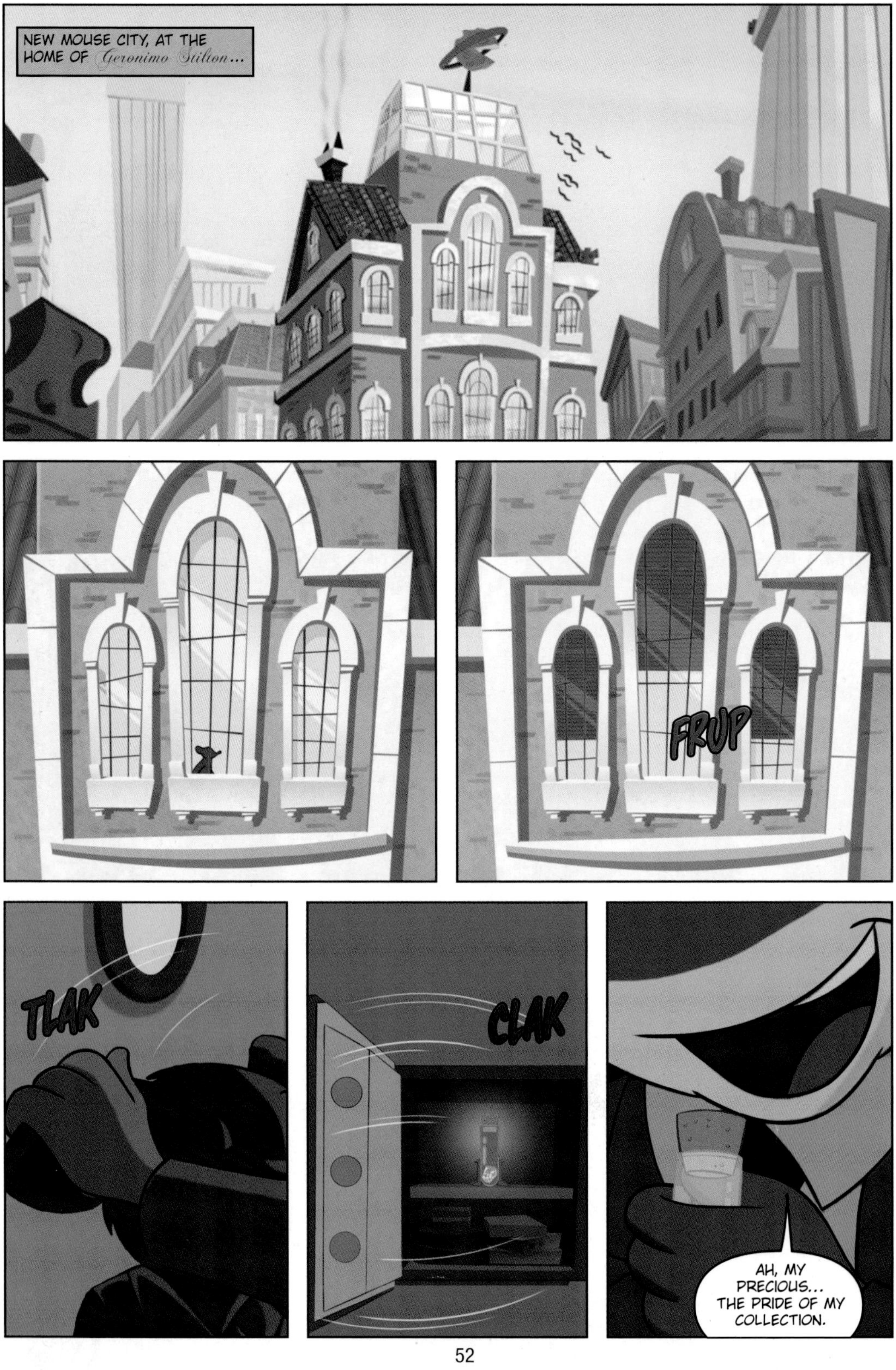
NEW MOUSE CITY, AT THE HOME OF Geronimo Stilton...
FRUP
TLAK
CLAK
AH, MY PRECIOUS... THE PRIDE OF MY COLLECTION.

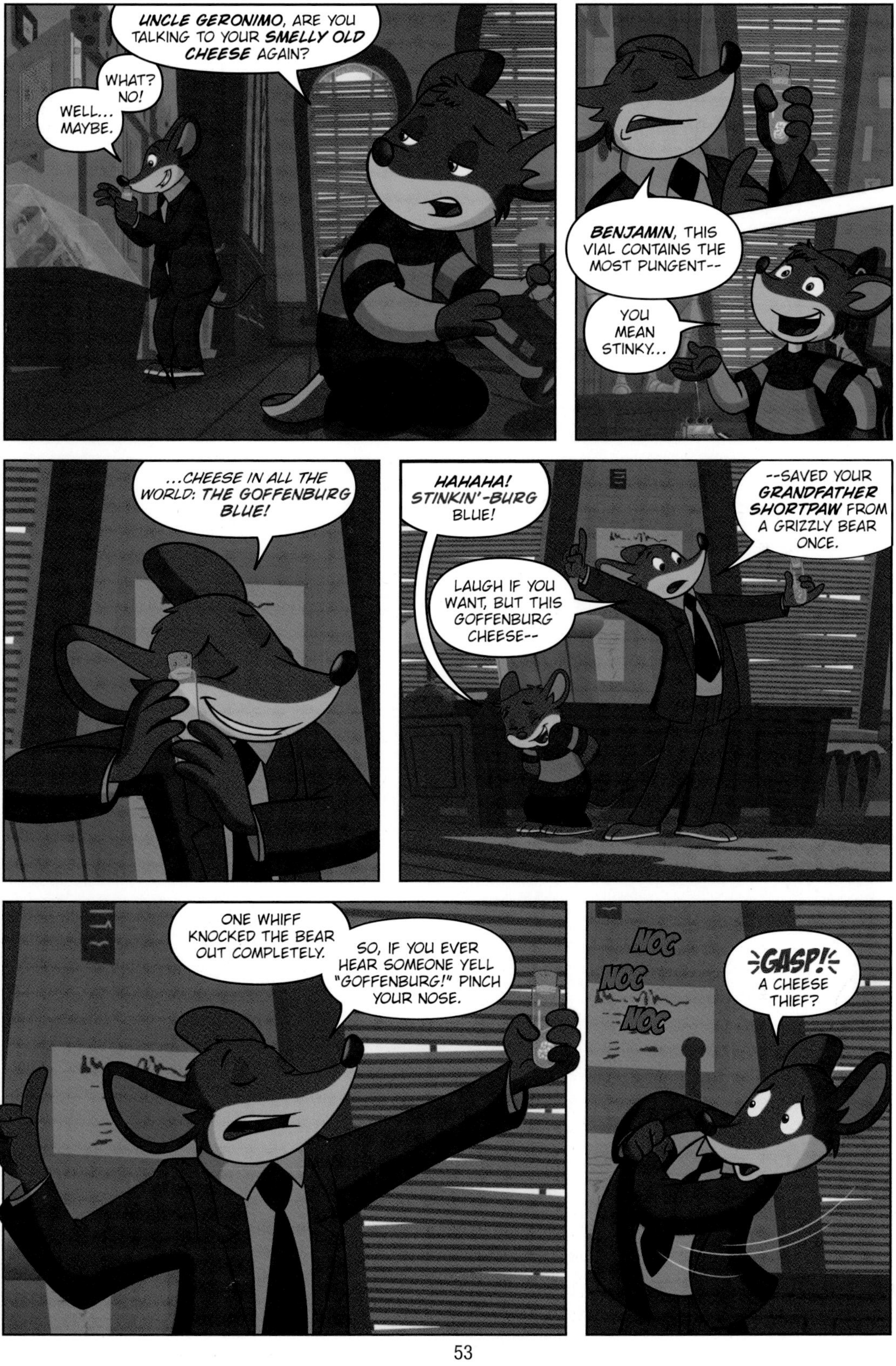
UNCLE GERONIMO, ARE YOU TALKING TO YOUR SMELLY OLD CHEESE AGAIN?
WHAT? NO!
WELL... MAYBE.
BENJAMIN, THIS VIAL CONTAINS THE MOST PUNGENT--
YOU MEAN STINKY...
...CHEESE IN ALL THE WORLD: THE GOFFENBURG BLUE!
HAHAHA! STINKIN'-BURG BLUE!
LAUGH IF YOU WANT, BUT THIS GOFFENBURG CHEESE--
--SAVED YOUR GRANDFATHER SHORTPAW FROM A GRIZZLY BEAR ONCE.
ONE WHIFF KNOCKED THE BEAR OUT COMPLETELY.
SO, IF YOU EVER HEAR SOMEONE YELL "GOFFENBURG!" PINCH YOUR NOSE.
NOC
NOC
NOC
GASP!
A CHEESE THIEF?

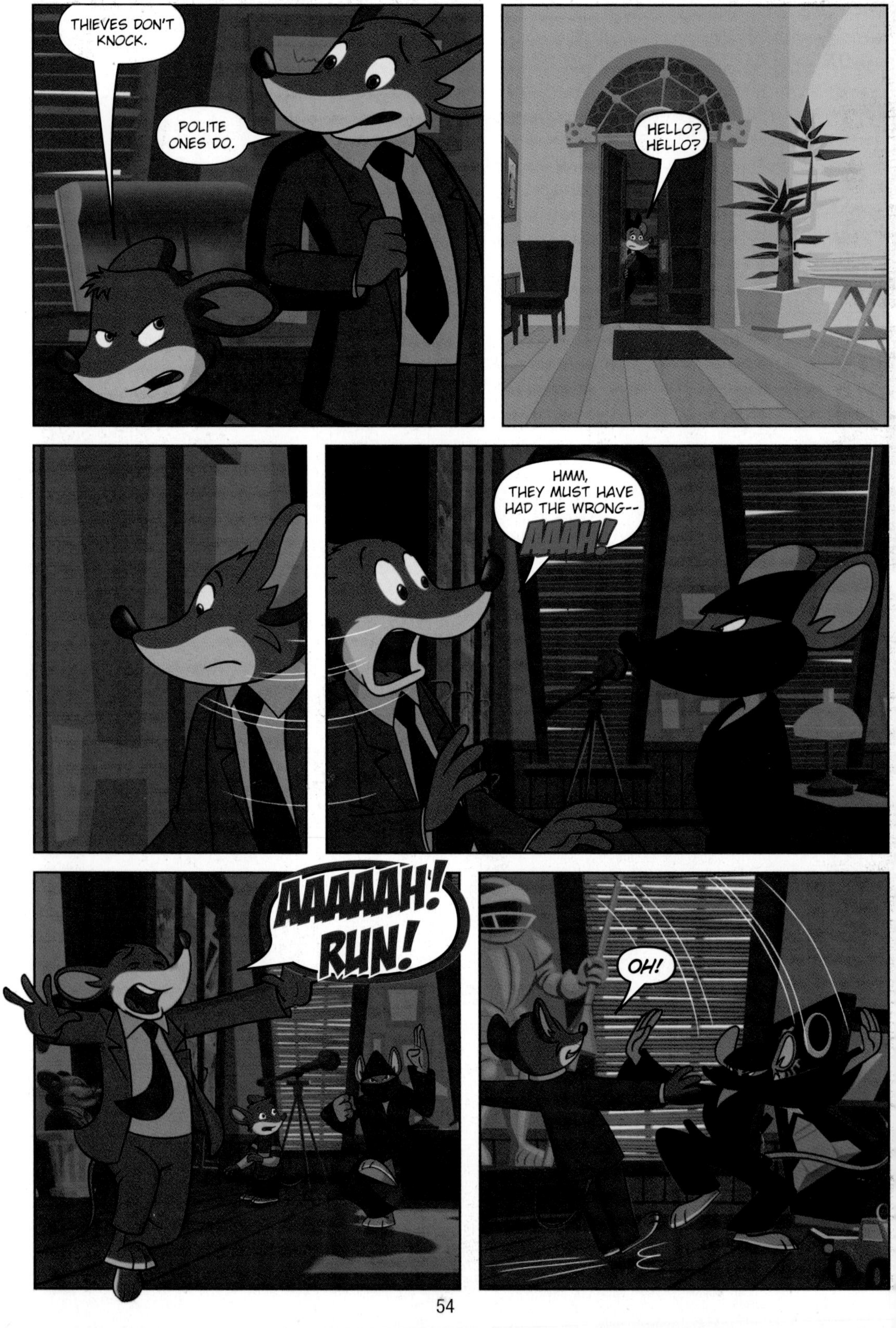
THIEVES DON'T KNOCK.
POLITE ONES DO.
HELLO? HELLO?
HMM, THEY MUST HAVE HAD THE WRONG--
AAAH!
AAAAAH! RUN!
OH!

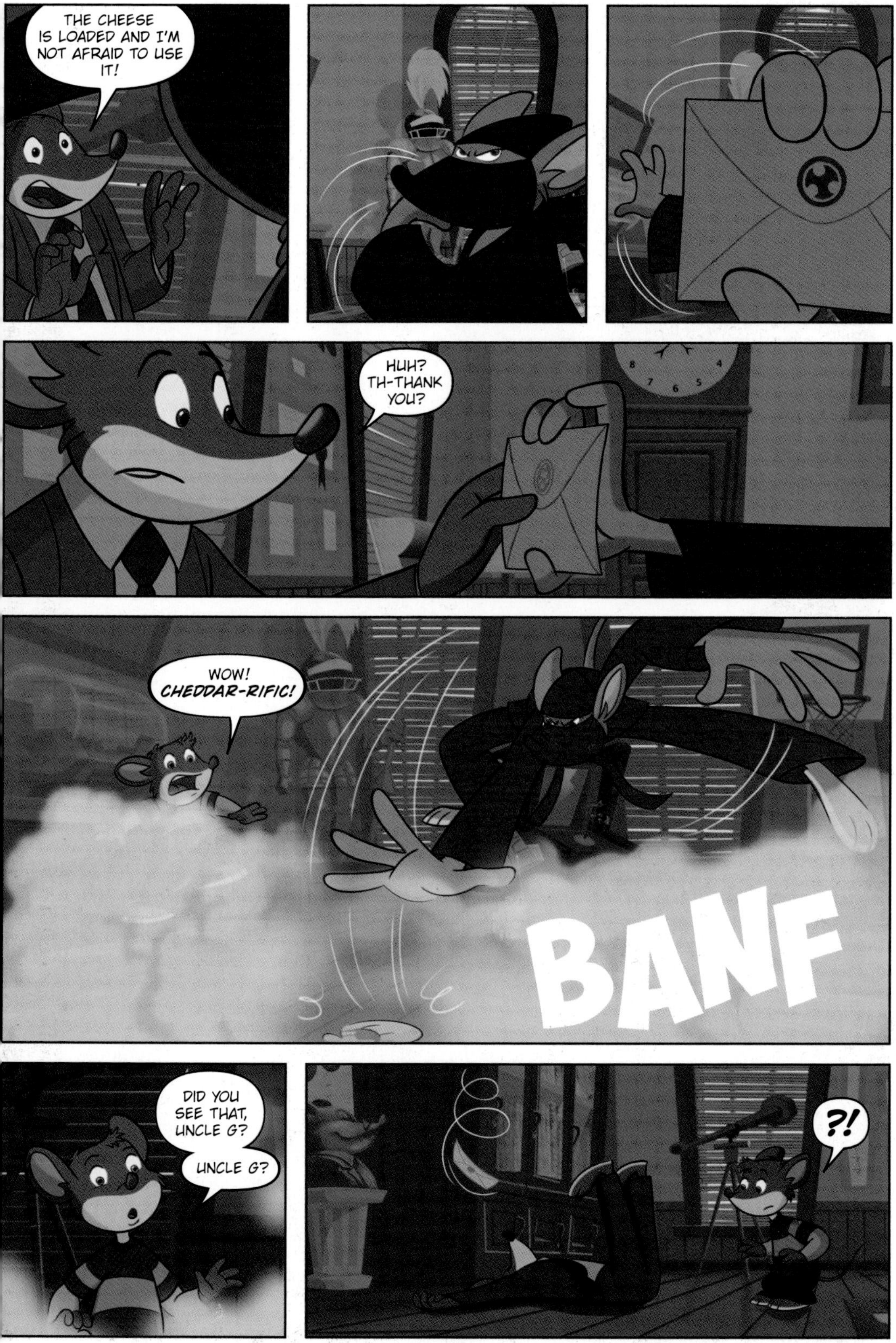
THE CHEESE IS LOADED AND I'M NOT AFRAID TO USE IT!
HUH? TH-THANK YOU?
WOW! CHEDDAR-RIFIC!
BANF
DID YOU SEE THAT, UNCLE G?
UNCLE G?
?!

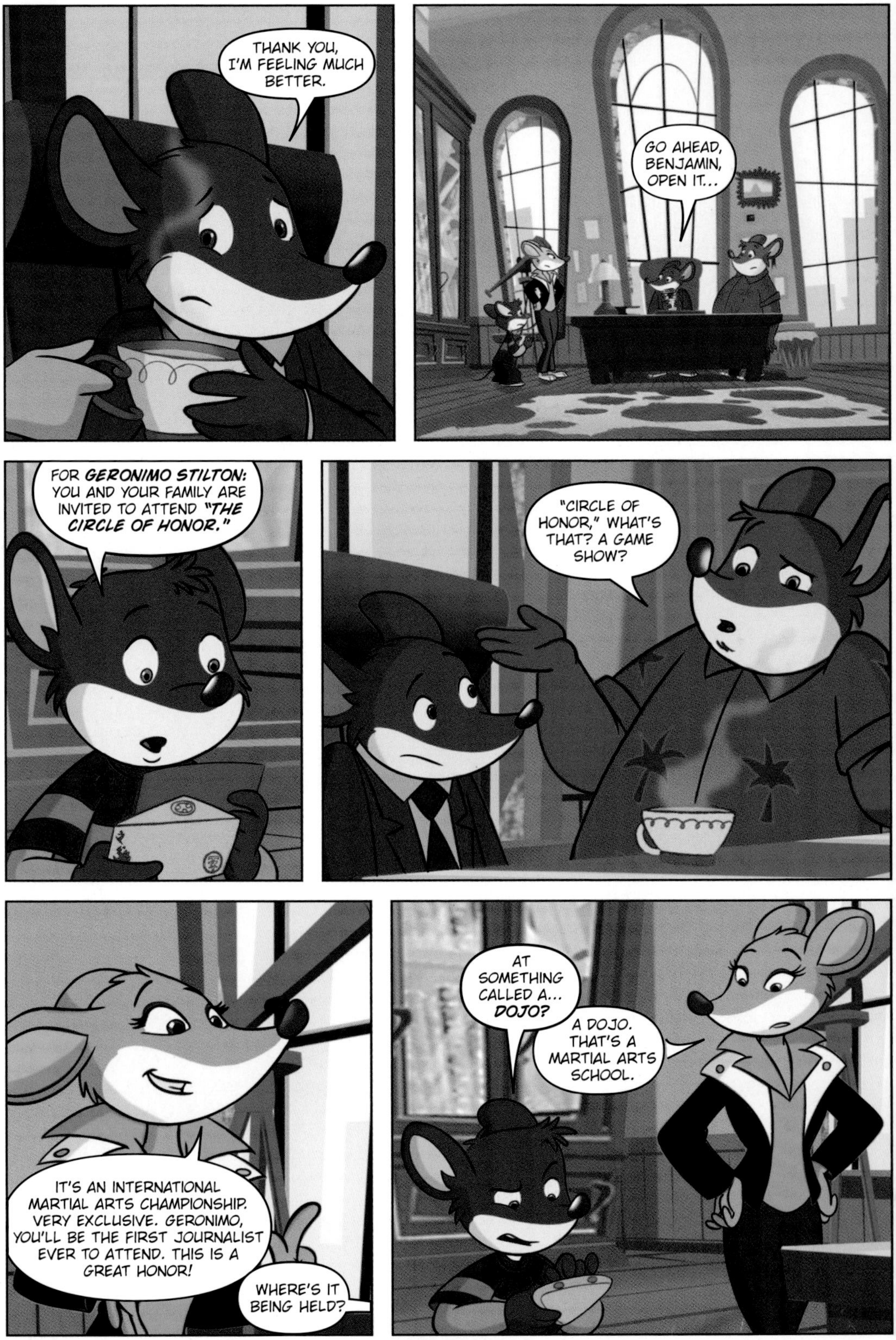
THANK YOU, I'M FEELING MUCH BETTER.
GO AHEAD, BENJAMIN, OPEN IT...
FOR GERONIMO STILTON: YOU AND YOUR FAMILY ARE INVITED TO ATTEND "THE CIRCLE OF HONOR."
"CIRCLE OF HONOR," WHAT'S THAT? A GAME SHOW?
IT'S AN INTERNATIONAL MARTIAL ARTS CHAMPIONSHIP. VERY EXCLUSIVE. GERONIMO, YOU'LL BE THE FIRST JOURNALIST EVER TO ATTEND. THIS IS A GREAT HONOR!
WHERE'S IT BEING HELD?
AT SOMETHING CALLED A... DOJO?
A DOJO. THAT'S A MARTIAL ARTS SCHOOL.

**Don't Miss GERONIMO STILTON REPORTER #9 "The Mask of Rat-Jitsu"!**
**Coming soon!**

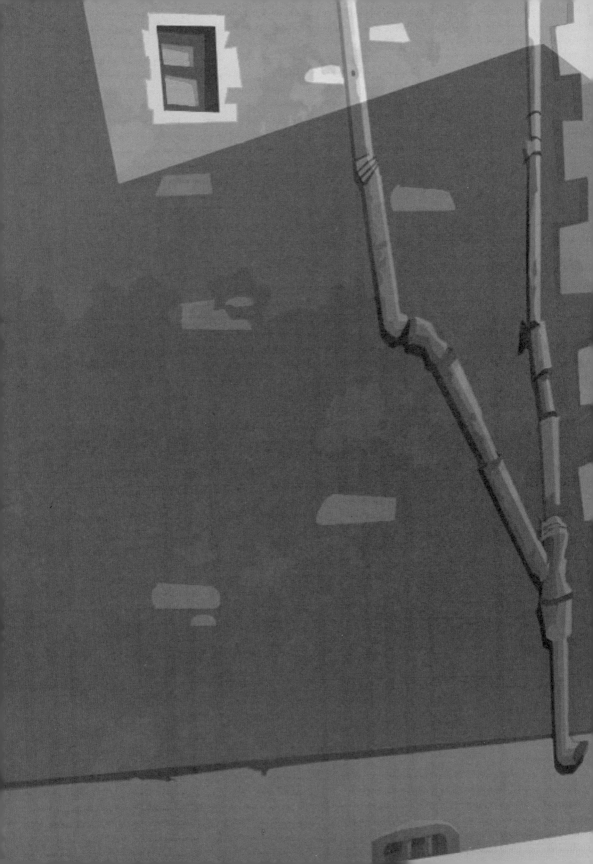